CADILLAC,
OKLAHOMA

CADILLAC, OKLAHOMA

Louise Farmer Smith

ISBN: 978-0-9964395-2-7

UPPER HAND PRESS
P. O. Box 91179
Bexley, Ohio 43209
U. S. A.

Designed by Natalee Michelle Brown

Printed at Bookmasters, Ashland, Ohio

For Tim and Virginia

ACKNOWLEDGMENTS

Sugar House, *Virginia Quarterly Review*,
Summer, 1997

The Soloist, *Antietam Review*, Fiction Prize, 1997

The Estate, *Weber Studies*, Summer, 1998

Deep and Comforting Voice, *Writers Forum*,
Winter, 1999

Faithful Elders, *Potomac Review*, Fiction Prize,
Fall, 2000

Don't Turn Around, anthologized in *Dots on a Map*,
Mint Hill Press, 2008

The American Mind, *Potomac Review*, Spring, 2010

Voice of Experience, *CrossTimbers*, 2012,
Pushcart nominee

For Tim and Virginia

The use of the surname, Willard, is a tribute to Sherwood Anderson.

VOICE OF EXPERIENCE
SLOANE ISAAC WILLARD
1948

Sally arrived in our town the summer I turned seventeen, and that three-month stretch of heat burned up what was left of my childhood. She had that kind of wrecked voice that made her sound like a pack-a-day smoker, a woman with a story to tell in what my granddad Sloane Benjamin Willard, who'd been to France in WWI, called a whiskey voice. She looked to me like she might be as old as twenty-five, the perfect older woman to train me for what I hoped would be a lifetime of pleasing women.

Earlier, in the spring, I'd made a very bad start on this with Mary Evelyn Huffman after the Junior prom, when I kissed her on the nose and not in a cute way. The look of disgust on Mary Evelyn's face said she could tell what a clumsy idiot I was. That had been the close of an almost interminable year, 1948, which yielded only one thing of any value. In American Lit class I read a quote from Benjamin Franklin about older women being grateful for the attentions of younger men. This, of course, was not a passage assigned by the teacher, but the fruit of my habitual prowling outside the designated pages looking for richer material.

Sally lived with relatives by the name of Lancaster, a kind but childless couple, whose only distinction in town was raising peacocks on a heavily treed acreage a mile or two west. I was surprised when Mother told me Sally had taken a job as the Methodist church secretary, and I let myself imagine that this job — keeping attendance records, paying utility bills, and writing notes to shut-ins — was a cover, a kind of recompense for the former, racy life her husky voice suggested. Sometimes I'd feel ashamed of this fantasy when I'd see her in town, modestly dressed and minding her own business. But she was one of the few good-looking single women in Cadillac, and I finally convinced myself that seeing as how I was from a good Baptist family, it would be a step in the right direction for her to get to know me.

I devised a plan. My summer job was making the deliveries for McCall's Grocery. I had fixed a large sturdy box to the front of my bicycle and pedaled around town in 90 plus degree heat trying to reach the housewives before the milk and eggs got warm. So it was easy for me to pedal over to the church office and pretend I had a delivery for the pastor.

Standing in the doorway, grinning, my tall gangly shadow making the little room even darker, I held up the bag of onions a housewife had changed her mind about.

"I'm Sloane Isaac Willard with your grocery delivery, ma'am." The office wasn't much more than a closet and smelled of dust. It was hot as hell. There was a high window in the back, but it looked like it was painted shut. Stacks of hymnals were stored on the floor. In the dim light Sally was typing at a table just big enough to hold the huge typewriter.

"I'm sorry. What did you say?" She looked at me politely, like maybe I wanted to join the church.

"You could use a fan in here."

"Did you need something?"

"Whatcha typing?"

"Reverend Morgan's sermon. Can I help you?"

Just hearing that tragic voice made me sure I'd chosen the right woman, but the fact that she was encircled by hymnals and typing a sermon set me back and I left.

It took a week to come up with a new plan. I spent all the tips I'd earned since the first of June to purchase a small black electric fan at the second-hand store. I hid it in the stock room at McCall's until I had a delivery in the direction of the church.

That night I overheard my aunt tell my mother that Sally had been married very briefly to what she described as a "clean-cut young man from a good family." The two women went on to speculate about what went wrong, and I pretended to shine my shoes.

"Perhaps he didn't want children," Mother offered.

"We-ell," said my aunt, always one to darken any discussion, "perhaps it was her who didn't want children."

"Nooo," Mother said. "Not that sweet thing. There she is working for Reverend Morgan. He wouldn't hire a woman who didn't want children."

"Three months they were married," my aunt said, her eyebrows up. "A woman always believes that she can bring a man around to children over the years. Right? But a man would act swiftly if his bride said, absolutely no children. No man would stick by a woman like that even though she is a pretty little thing."

My whole body was heating up at the idea of Sally having been married, and my mind pressed her against the wall of the church office. "I'll just finish these on the back porch," I told the women as I clutched my shoes in front of my zipper.

When I took the fan to Sally, I insisted that she let me plug it in. With the seriousness of a man installing an electric washing machine, I instructed her to sit at her desk while I sat on the floor and adjusted the direction of the airflow until it fluttered her skirt. Still sitting on the floor, I schooled her on the importance of using the oscillating option. "You want the fan to blow away from you for a second or two, so you can start to sweat again. That makes it cooler when the fan hits you." She nodded politely and thanked me, her husky voice making me sweat even more. I gazed at the bare pink toes in her sandals until she said, "Now that I have all this cool air, I know my work will go faster. Thank you again. That was very sweet."

This was as close as I'd been and if I left now, I had no idea what I'd do next to get inside this room. I backed two steps to the door. "Do you have a car?" I blurted.

She put her head to the side like she was on to me.

"Never mind," I said, "I just wondered how you got to work and back out to the Lancasters."

"Sometimes I have a ride. Sometimes I walk. It's not very far."

"Seems far to me. A mile or two."

She shrugged and turned to her work.

The sting of this rejection sent me into a week of despair mixed with moments of wild elation. The image of the married woman pressed the accelerator on my heart, and I prayed for inspiration. Meanwhile, I decided to attend the Methodist services. The next Sunday, I sat directly behind her. That was a mistake. I could smell her flowery fragrance and was soon in no condition to be in the company of God and the Methodists.

Nights were torture. My mind would fly into extravagant fantasies of running away with her, me improbably at the wheel of the Lancaster's Dodge, and then everything would crash in sweaty, unsatisfying attempts to satisfy myself. I slept little and my parents eyed me with suspicion and concern.

From behind the parsonage's forsythia hedge, I spied on Sally and discovered that she left the church every day at 3:00 on the dot. My deliveries were usually over by 2:00 and the obvious solution finally dawned on me. Route 201, the road to the Lancaster's, opened before me, the path to Paradise.

Clean and pressed, I showed up at 3:00 Friday afternoon to walk her home. She was putting a stiff, black cover on her typewriter. "You're in high school, aren't you." It wasn't a question. "You're the druggist's boy."

I nodded. "Sloane Isaac Willard, ma'am," and added that I was a senior and liked walking and talking. I let on that I was well-read in current events and literature and had a lot to talk about. She shrugged. And we began our first walk together.

I talked about the Marshall Plan. I talked about President Truman and a whole lot of other stuff I've forgotten now. A nervous kid talking big and not stopping to take a breath, I didn't inquire about her, where she came from, or what she liked. When the Lancaster's farm suddenly loomed before me, I realized I'd wasted my first opportunity to learn anything from this woman or make myself desirable to her. She thanked me for seeing her home, an old-fashioned phrase even then, and the gulf between our ages widened.

There's always a price to pay for trying something

16

new in a small town, and sure enough, a friend of my aunt had seen us as she'd driven past. The sound of the car had probably been drowned out by the raving idiot who hadn't noticed.

"Aren't you getting a little ahead of yourself?" my aunt asked in a voice overflowing with insinuation. "Why don'tcha tell that girl she needs to clear her throat."

"Margaret!" said my mother, always one to protect me. "Did you know that McCall's put their mayonnaise on sale?"

"No one else in this town has much to say," Sally said after we'd started walking regularly, and I'd calmed down. "To me, I mean," she added.

I thought about this, then asked, "Haven't you made any friends here?"

"I get the idea that a divorced woman is a little suspect."

In one fell swoop Sally had opened up a real conversation. I felt I was in way over my head and just listened to our footsteps on the gravelly shoulder of the road. Finally I asked, "What's it like, getting divorced?"

She turned her head away. "Divorce is just a legal term. It doesn't mean you stop loving someone."

This was unexpected. I wanted a story about a rotten guy who hit her, and she was too proud to stay with such a man and got a lawyer. "So why'd you get divorced? Didn't he want children?"

"We both wanted children very much." The farm was in sight and she thanked me and took off, walking fast. I watched her head for that house where two dull, old people waited, people who hadn't, as my mother had reported, introduced her to potential friends at their church. But I didn't want her to have friends. I needed her to be so desperately lonely that she'd value the company of a high school boy.

By the end of July the heat stayed through the night, the leaves on the trees drooped, and the grass turned straw color as usual. Sometimes Mr. Lancaster was waiting out in front of the church in his Dodge, so I didn't get to walk Sally home. But when I did, she smiled like she was glad to see me. My aunt kept teasing me about the divorcée, but that got easier to ignore. I also gained a little more control of the conversation with Sally.

"What was it like being married?" I asked near the end of August.

"He's a wonderful man." Her voice caressed the words, and I despaired. At least she hadn't given his name. I didn't really want to know anything about him. I just wanted to know her. "So why did you get divorced?"

She didn't say anything for most of a mile, and my heart ached a little for her because I knew some big thing had happened to her, and she'd had to leave her hometown and had no one to talk to. No way to work it out of her system.

She gave me a sad look. "You're so young."

"Oh Sally, don't say that. Just talk to me. You know you'll feel better if you talk to me."

She thought about this for another quarter mile, then without any prompting from me said, "I didn't want to leave him, and his parents said if I stayed with him, they'd put me through school at the university. Pay for everything." She glanced at me to see how I was taking this.

"You loved him. You wanted to stay. You could have had a college education. So?" I could have mentioned I'd heard he was clean-cut and from a good family, too, but she was praising him enough, and besides it would hurt her to know she was talked about.

"Let's rest a minute," she said. There was a big cottonwood tree surrounded by bushes on the right side of the road, and we sat down in some dead grass beneath the tree. We were close enough to the farm that I could hear one of the peacocks screaming, like the squall of a wildcat.

Sally sat down, pulled her dress down tight over her bent knees and crossed her arms around them. Looking off toward town, she rested her chin on her arms. "I left Stillwater because I couldn't bear to run into Stephen. Just seeing him burned a hole in me. I couldn't live with him in the same house and not really have him as my husband. Don't you see?"

"Didn't he love you?"

"He will always love me."

I didn't want to hear any more about these people. Wasn't love what made it all work? What had happened to her? She was so small and in so much pain. I put my arm around her and leaned my head against hers. "I'd do anything for you," I said.

She turned and put her hands on my chest and pressed me to the ground and let her slender body down on me. I got my arms around her. I knew what to do. She didn't have to tell me. One hand behind her head and the other across her back so as not to hurt her, I rolled us over. She had two hands full of my shirt. She was trembling. "I begged him!" she cried. She had wanted Stephen and he hadn't wanted her, and her body bucked with the grief of this. "Please," she sobbed and I slid my hand up between her legs but she pushed me away and sat up, leaned her head on her knees and sobbed. Though I was burning, I sat up and rested my hand on her back. Panting, I waited.

Finally Sally turned to me. "I'm sorry. I'm so sorry. It's just I always thought Stephen would be the first."

What could I say? I'd been so close. Life would never bring me another woman like Sally. I swallowed hard. "It's okay," I muttered and softly patted her back. "It's okay. But I can't imagine a man not wanting you, so maybe he was queer? Was that it?"

"Don't tell anyone."

"I won't." I flushed under this sign of her trust.

"I couldn't figure out what was wrong with me." She began to cry again.

"Oh, Sally, nothing, nothing in the world is wrong with you. You just need a different man. One who'll love you completely."

"You think I'll find one?"

"Sure you will."

She sniffed and with a sad little smile she said, "So will Stephen." Then she began to really cry.

"I guess so." Now I wanted to cry 'cause I'd lost my chance, but also because I knew I sure hadn't been offering real love.

"You'll find a girl," she said. "And she'll be so lucky to have a boy who is driven to pursue and win her."

That day I took her words as a promise that I would find a girl to love, and through the years I've always been grateful that whatever she thought of her clumsy, relentless suitor, she never laughed at him. Now, nearly seventy years on, my youth seems like a foreign country, a place where a deranged young man could carry on his secret mission in a town that neither enriched nor stunted its children.

Some of the details of Sally's unique prettiness have

faded, but not the memory of us sitting there under the cottonwood, two virgins picking grass out of each other's hair, me and the woman who taught me about love.

§

THE ESTATE
SLOANE ISAAC WILLARD
2012

My name is Phoebe and I was eleven the winter of 2012, so I got to sit with the grownups in the pew next to my Great Uncle, Sloane Willard. It was an easy funeral. Nobody had to come too far or cry too hard, though I did feel Uncle Sloane sighing and swallowing during the service. It was his half-brother Wendell who had died.

But afterwards at his big place, he sliced the ham with the stately calm we expected from him. He was my favorite relative, a person I could count on when something funny happened at the dinner table — like Marvella claiming Grover Richmond had proposed to her, something an eleven-year-old like me wasn't supposed to understand anyway. I'd look over at Sloane and see him drop his jaw without opening his mouth and give me a sideways, big-eyed look.

He was old now and given to staring spells, and on top of that he was probably the most grieved of us all by his younger brother's dying. Wendell had taken up farming after retiring from the railroad. "Wendell's talent is for telegraphy," Sloane used to say when people laughed about Wendell's farm. His cows, Patsy and

Opal, went dry because Uncle Wendell was too shy to take them to the neighbor's bull. He kept the dry cows on as pets. And he kept everything else he'd inherited with the farm—the rusting plows and harrows, the dead tractors and combines, the many hoops of wire and bales of fencing—scattered about the place just as he'd found them. Wendell was kind of the opposite of Uncle Sloane, who was a lawyer.

We all relied on Uncle Sloane to know what to do after the funeral. Minnie, his sister-in-law, a widow who lived with her nephew, had on her brown dotted Sunday dress and laid on the ham, black-eyed peas, biscuits, and green beans. She put all this on Uncle Sloane's long dining table along with all the Jell-O salads, banana cakes and pies the neighbors had brought in.

Everyone came—my family, all the Mullinses and Marvella. After dinner Mother sat down in the rocker with the baby, and the twins fell asleep in Dad's lap. Ted and Nelva Mullins were stuffed and collapsed on the big Victorian furniture in the parlor. The whole family hardly moved except the Mullins boys, who were scuffling under the dining room table, and Marvella, Sloane's niece.

A woman about my mother's age, Marvella, was Uncle Sloane's closest and least favorite relative. I figured this out from listening. No one knew all the things I'd figured out except Sloane. He always saw me listening. And he gave me a glance now when Marvella brought up the Hutschenreuther plates.

"I wonder who'll get the plates?" she said, addressing the lampshade next to her. She had on her purple suit with a lavender flower stitched on the shoulder in a permanent corsage. She'd done her hair a more innocent blond for the funeral.

"What plates?" It was Ted Mullins' wife, Nelva, her face pulled tight by her skinned back hair; the rest of her was fat—soft and white and slick as Crisco. Ted Mullins was basically the same shape as his wife except his head was put on low, so his shoulders rose up behind his ears. Ted was Marvella's second cousin. He and his wife and four kids had driven over from Seminole for the funeral.

"The Hutschenreuther plates, of course," said Marvella fingering the lavender buttons down the hip of the tight suit. "The only thing of value the poor man had."

Nelva Mullins pulled forward in the easy chair and her skirt rode up, showing large white knees above the rolled hose. "How valuable?" she asked.

Marvella ducked her head modestly, too polite, I guess, to discuss money. "Well goodness, I wouldn't know," she said, running a painted red nail along the edge of the big lavender flower. "The value of antiques goes up all the time, and these have been in our family for generations. Sloane's granddaddy bought them in St. Louis. But when Wendell promised them to me, I did just

25

happen to ask a friend in the business what they might be worth, in general terms, but that was several years ago."

"Yeah?" Nelva Mullins said, pushing hard on the arms of the chair to keep her weight from sliding her back. "How much? In general terms?"

"Well, of course, it's the sentimental value, something from the family, all those Christmas dinners for so many years—"

Nelva glared at Marvella.

"If the plates are perfect," Marvella said, "perhaps fifty dollars a plate."

"Good grief. How many are there?" Nelva asked.

"A perfect dozen, last time Uncle Wendell and I counted them. The day he promised them to me."

"Ted?" Nelva said accusingly.

"I never heard anything about plates." His chin on his chest, he was just beginning to doze off after his second piece of pecan pie.

"Don't you think, Sloane," she asked, "we ought to have the reading of the will now?"

Sloane had just gotten up to move a cut glass vase off a rather small table a couple of the Mullins boys were dodging around. He looked over at Marvella. "Why?"

"Well because," Marvella said, "the Mullinses have come a long way. It'd just mean another trip with these poor children if they had to come back."

"I would not be offended," Sloane said, "if they left

the children home when they come for the reading of the will."

"Sloane, there is no sense in that," Marvella whined. "We are all here. Sloane?"

He'd bent his knees to squint out the side window toward the driveway. Marvella probably thought he was having a staring spell and let herself go back to tormenting Nelva about the plates. Sloane plucked my sleeve, and we went outside through the back stairs hall.

When I saw the man standing beside his car, wringing his hands and saying, "Sloane, Sloane, I am so very sorry for this," I thought he was a mourner come too late for the funeral. He looked much younger than Dad but had a bald head and a fat face, and with his hands clasped in front of his zipper, his whole soft body kept swaying with apology. "Sloane, if my daddy knew I was doing this to you on the day of Wendell's funeral, he would just throw me right out of the firm, and I won't blame you if you tell him, but—"

"What's up, Randolph?"

It was chilly out, and Sloane turned up the collar of his suit coat, put his arm around me, and set our backs to the wind. The man was holding out his hand toward a young woman standing on the other side of the car, and from the fearful look in her eye, she wasn't about to come around to our side. She looked like a shy high school girl in a waitress uniform.

"Sloane, I should have called you. I should have called you weeks ago," the man said.

"It's cold out here, Randolph. What is it?"

"And now the funeral and all the relatives here. I was afraid you might read out an old will and things would be even worse." The man took a deep breath and wrung his hands. "Wendell made another will."

A will? This man was a lawyer, too.

"So?" said Sloane.

"Her!" the lawyer said looking guilty. "Her! He gave it all to her."

The girl pulled her shrunk up old blue sweater around her and looked away.

"Who is she?" Sloane asked.

The lawyer now stepped closer to us so the girl couldn't hear and whispered, "She's a manicurist."

"A what?" Sloane cupped his hand behind his good ear.

"That girl was giving Wendell manicures."

Sloane leaned forward and squinted into the face of the much shorter man. "Are you telling me that my brother was getting his fingernails painted?"

"No, no, Sloane, just buffed up, probably, maybe the cuticle—"

"Men don't do that in this town, Randolph."

"Sure they do, Sloane, down at the barbershop, a few, the banker—"

28

"Wendell was not the banker. The man didn't get a haircut more that three or four times a year. He didn't like barbers."

"She doesn't work at the barber shop. She works over at Parisian Lady."

"Randolph, you are impinging upon my credulity as well as my hospitality—"

"See! That's why it was so hard to call you in the first place. I don't know how they met, but the shampoo girl told my wife that after all the customers were gone, old Wendell would come around to the back door and she'd," he nodded toward the manicurist, "let him in, and well, they'd sit at a little table in the back and talk while she—you know, soaked his fingers and—"

Randolph kept leaning closer and wincing and giving me dark looks. "Well, you know," he said, "lotion and stuff, and a few weeks ago he came to my office and told me she was all alone with two young kids and asked me to make him a will leaving her his place. Now I'm sure that's all it was, just the manicures, but now it's his property, and for me to have to come over here at a time of grieving—" Randolph shifted his weight and reclasped his hands.

"A man," Sloane said, "has a right to bequeath his property as he sees fit. Did you make the will?"

"Yes, sir, and I should have called you. When your niece, Marvella Ketcham, gets wind of this, there's going

29

to be a real donnybrook."

"And did he sign it?"

"Yes, sir."

"And do you have it with you?"

Randolph took a tan envelope out from inside his coat and handed it to Sloane. "I am so sorry," he said.

Sloane took the will, and we walked around to the other side of the car. The girl backed away from us and turned a little to the side. I could see that her socks had crawled down into her bunged-up white shoes. Her face was thin, with blue gray circles under the eyes.

"Who was your husband, ma'am?" Sloane asked.

"Tommy Jarrett," she said softly. "He got hisself smothered down at the grain elevator."

"I'm sorry to hear that, ma'am."

"And now I lost Wendell. I'm just bad luck for men." She put her hand over her mouth.

"Wendell was seventy-eight," Sloane said.

"That's right, sir, thank you."

Sloane opened the car door for her. Randolph trotted around the car and cupped his hand as though to keep the girl from hearing. "I don't need to tell you how it's going to be, Sloane. Sure as shooting. Once the relatives start squabbling, the gossips in this town will just blow this thing up bigger than— Then I don't know how you'll keep all that beauty parlor information from O'Brian at *The Courier* which will—"

"Randolph." Sloane raised a hand to stop the sputtering. "Would you take Mrs. Jarrett home, please? I'll call on you in your office Monday morning."

And that was that. Sloane was silent as we walked toward the house, and he patted me on the back as if to say don't worry, but he wasn't looking at me at all. We ducked into the back bedroom and he told me to close the door and stand watch. After puffing out a long breath, he sat down at his desk, opened up the will and gave it a quick look. Then he put it in the drawer, and sat awhile frowning at his desk. Finally, he took out a sheet of paper and began to write.

I listened at the door and could only hear Minnie cleaning up the kitchen and Ted Mullins snoring. The kids were running around in the yard, and I guessed everyone else was taking it easy.

After he got done writing, Sloane sent me to get Minnie out of the kitchen. She took off her apron and brought a kitchen chair into the living room for herself. The others began to wake up. Mother stood up with the baby and shook down her dress, and Dad yawned and adjusted the sleeping twins. Ted and Nelva shifted and blinked in their easy chairs. Marvella got out her compact and gave her new blond do a push or two. I could see her looking past her little mirror to give Ted and Nelva dirty looks.

Sloane took a seat in his big armchair, and I settled on

the arm beside him. "This is not Wendell's will," Sloane began when everyone was paying attention. "This is a précis of his intentions."

"What do you mean a pray-see?" Marvella was getting her back up already.

Sloane dipped his chin and glared over his glasses at her. "There is a lot of useless legal language in the will itself. This is just a summary of it, the who-gets-what of it, Marvella."

"All right," she said.

"To Alice," Sloane began. My mother looked up in mild surprise. " — in whose kitchen I have drunk a thousand of cups of coffee, I leave the china cup and saucer her mother painted."

"Oh, goodness," Mother's eyes got teary and she bit her lip. "I had no idea he would remember."

"To my cousin, Ted Mullins, I leave all my farm implements."

"Farm implements!" Nelva shouted. "There isn't nothing out there that wasn't rusted all to heck twenty years ago!"

Ted Mullins patted his wife's hand, leaned over and said, "Scrap iron, Nelva."

Sloane looked over his glasses at Ted. "Can you take care of this?"

"You bet." Ted dipped his low head. "I figure six, eight truck loads. Just have to take Monday off."

Nelva raised a superior smile in Marvella's direction. She knew that six or eight truckloads of scrap iron beat out twelve perfect plates no matter how much they'd appreciated. Marvella clasped her hands on the purple skirt, pursed her lips and concentrated anew on Sloane.

Sitting on the arm of his chair I could read his elegant, spidery handwriting, so I was surprised when he said, "To Minnie, my sister-in-law, I leave my kitchen clock."

Minnie, perched on the kitchen chair, jerked her chin and began to blink and look about in that clucky hen way of hers. "Kitchen clock?" she asked. "I don't ever remember Wendell having a kitchen clock, do you, Alice? Marvella? A kitchen clock?"

"I believe this was a gift to him from someone," Sloane said. "I doubt he ever took it out of the box."

"Oh," Minnie said, "well, that would explain it." She folded her hands in her lap and sank again into stillness. Then her whole body jerked. "But did any of you give him a kitchen clock, I mean if you did, and you want it back—Alice? Nelva? Marvella?"

"I don't believe," Marvella said, "I can recall ever actually giving him a clock, at least not for the kitchen. Does it say specifically, kitchen clock?"

"Yes," Sloane snapped, "and it says it goes to Minnie, his sister-in-law."

Sloane then cleared his throat and adjusted his glasses. Suspense settled on the group, and he took up reading something that was actually on the page. "To my beloved niece, Marvella, I leave the plates."

"Ohhh," Marvella sobbed, "that sweet old man, that sweet, sweet old man." The relief of it all took her, and she bent over her hankie and bawled.

There was one more item on the sheet of paper that Sloane held. He cleared his throat again to hush up Marvella and proceeded. "My land and house and furniture I leave to the orphans of my young friend whose life was snuffed out so early, Tommy Jarrett."

"Ohhh," Marvella began again, "isn't that sweet." Nothing could diminish her happiness. I knew that more than the plates, she had noticed that she was the only one called beloved. And now to have received her bequest within a will that stooped to care for orphans only increased her joy.

Sloane folded the paper and everyone in the room rose as if they were floating up on clouds. Minnie brought the coats and covered dishes of leftovers for each family, and everyone kissed goodbye, especially Marvella, who couldn't seem to get enough kissing and hugging. She kept right on crying as she went out the door.

Mother bundled up the baby, and I got the little kids into their coats while Dad warmed up the car.

"Uncle Sloane," I whispered as the others were trooping out the door. "You made all that up."

He pulled his chin down and looked at me over

his glasses.

"And besides, Mother said you looked after Uncle Wendell all his life. He should have left it all to you."

Sloane was looking at me but not saying anything. Then he glanced out the door at the rest of the folks at the curb. "Sometimes," he said, "a brother—" He heaved a big sigh and placed his fingertips on the mahogany hall table. "Let's just say, sometimes trying for justice is—is simply too ambitious, and—" It wasn't like Sloane to sigh, staring at the floor, his eyes big behind his glasses. I waited 'til he went on. "And if you can't get justice, well then, you try for peace."

I wasn't sure what he was saying. All fall I'd felt so good about being eleven, almost grown up, but now it looked like being a grown up was a sad thing, and even being a smart man like Sloane didn't make it easy.

"You didn't get anything either," he said in his old jokey voice.

"Yeah, but I'm only a child."

§

"This bunch could use some leadership," Wynona Blosser whispered to herself as she eyed the Cadillac town fathers gathered around the long collapsible table in the low-ceilinged, windowless conference room under the Chamber of Commerce offices. The decision makers were here: Mayor Mashburn; his lawyer, Gavin McCall, who had for some reason brought his little, red-headed wife; the city manager; the city engineer; the manager of the electric company; and of course, herself, essential to this project as the president of the bank that would do the financing. That new reporter, O'Brian from The Cadillac Courier, who asked to come, had definitely been told, no. This was not a public meeting. Also present, of course, was Peanuts Murphy, the owner of the land the city was trying to buy. Sloane Willard, a retired lawyer, who for some reason carried a lot of weight in this town, had been invited by the mayor but said he had a conflict.

Since the late 70s — and this ground Wynona's spirit down every time she looked out the window of her office at the bank — the land in question had included an abandoned pool hall and a falling-down bowling alley. The owner of these shabby properties had rented out the yards around these derelict establishments for open storage of scrap iron and used plumbing fixtures.

The problem tonight was that the mayor was allowing the city engineer to drone on about the possibility of toxicity in the soil under these eye sores, which occupied two city blocks in the center of town. Wynona crossed her legs to hold onto her patience.

At the start of this meeting she had made it perfectly clear what the group was supposed to accomplish: Buy the land. Cadillac had the opportunity to distinguish itself among Oklahoma towns by creating within its heart a town green on the model of a New England commons. The centerpiece, Wynona had said, would be a Victorian ice cream parlor surrounded by a garden containing a large, gazebo-like bandstand. All this group needed to do was to come to an agreement with Peanuts Murphy on the price of the land.

Oh, good grief! Gavin McCall's wife kept asking the engineer questions about the soil. Wynona huffed and crossed her legs the other way. "Mrs. McCall," Wynona interrupted trying to sound sweet, "maybe you could satisfy your curiosity about the soil some other time. This is a meeting to arrange a real estate transaction."

The scrawny little thing stood up like everyone wanted to hear from her. "Mrs. Blosser," she said, "the town should not make a deal for land it will never be able to build on, especially a park where it would be unhealthy for children to play." The girl remained standing.

"Listen, Judy, honey—" Wynona started.

"My name is Judianne."

"Listen, Judianne. In case you hadn't noticed, what the town has right now are two falling-down buildings and a pile of toilets. Now is that the healthy playground our children deserve?"

"Esthetically it's a crime, but the EPA will shut down your project if this land turns out to be a toxic waste site."

Her husband yanked on her arm. "Judianne! Sit down," he hissed, but the woman tugged her arm out of her husband's grasp and said, "We need to think of the children."

"You don't even have any children!" Wynona shot back. It looked like that shut up the red-head, who slid away from her husband the lawyer. "All I'm saying," the little gal said softly, "is that the town should go ahead and authorize the testing of a soil sample." Then she did sit down, but not next to her handsome husband.

"If I could just return everybody's attention to the work to be done tonight," Wynona said. "No other town in Oklahoma has a dump in its business district. This is 2013. We are well into the 21st century and need to create something Cadillac can be proud of." She had everyone's attention now. She sensed her gold jewelry glittering in the fluorescent lights and felt the full power as the banker's widow, leading the way to beautiful, gracious living.

But suddenly, from the other end of the conference table, Peanuts Murphy, the crotchety owner of the property, croaked, "Let's get down to brass tacks here, folks. I own the property. Period."

"Which should have been condemned years ago," Wynona murmured so all could hear. Ever since a visit to New England when she was a young English teacher, Wynona had held a sense of romance for the villages she and a girlfriend had driven through—the pristine white churches on hillsides, the welcoming inns where open fires took the chill off late August nights. Returning to a 90-degree classroom in Cadillac, she vowed her days in Oklahoma were numbered, but at the end of that year Floyd Blosser, Sr., who was 43 and owned the bank, asked for her hand. She was so impressed with herself, landing this big fish, that she had floated right into marriage.

No one disagreed that the town should buy Peanuts' land and develop it. Least of all Peanuts, who had grown old watching his two favorite enterprises dwindle and finally become embarrassments. Wynona and everyone else knew his original motivation for the pool hall in the 60s was to draw the buddies that his personality had failed to attract. But over time he began to smell rank disrespect. He tossed out young jerks and finally threw a lock on the door to show them who was boss. The bowling alley, built to attract an older crowd, was extinguished in 1988 by the twelve-lane Bowl-a-Rama out at the mall.

Peanuts owned other buildings in Cadillac, the ones that housed the Laundra-mat, the Copy Shop, the Busy Bee Café, and Laces and Things, but these offered no love. He'd had two wives; the first left after three years of orthodontia achieved for her a smile that convinced her she could do better than Peanuts Murphy. The second wife, a dancer he'd wooed for forty-eight hours in Las Vegas, refused to leave town with him. No one in Cadillac would have had to know about his bride's reluctance to make a home in Cadillac, but the best man at the wedding, Chub Widmer, told all. And the town laughed and laughed until a sewer line broke, flooding the streets of a new housing addition, and the resulting scandal took the heat off Peanuts.

When neither party to the Las Vegas marriage contacted the other, Peanuts became comfortable with his ambiguous marital status and enjoyed the freedom of a bachelor who could whip out a glitzy, dog-eared marriage license whenever the kind of woman who would not improve his status in Cadillac tried to get serious. As the decades passed, Peanuts forgot his wedding-day humiliation and began to speak affectionately of his Las Vegas bride.

"I'd be thinking about a will," his friend R.J. had once said. "I mean, is she gonna inherit your money?"

Peanuts' eyes had lit up. "I'd sure like to see Wynona Blosser's face when she gets a load of my little Vegas whore reviving the pool hall." But he forgot the will. He had plans.

Tonight, Peanuts knew he was going to get top dollar from the city and what was more important, his ideas and his name were going to be all over this project from the get-go. That ice cream place was going to be the first of a franchise. He could see it plain as day, swanky architecture on the line of Denny's, and not just ice cream—a big menu with pictures so you could see what you were getting, and pretty waitresses, no fat girls. And there was plenty of room for a spacious parking lot. The place would glow in the night with blue neon along the roofline and a revolving sign on top, PEANUTS' PLACE.

The report of the city engineer finally droned to a halt.

"Now listen here!" Peanuts exploded from his end of the table, his aging spine curved further, an armadillo ready for battle. "That was just a lot of Whatifs from a guy who hasn't got any evidence what-so-ever. Right?" Peanuts glared at the city engineer who stared at the table.

Mayor Mashburn called on the manager of the utilities company to say what concessions Oklahoma Gas and Electric would make for this new city project.

"Sounds nice," the OGE manager said, "especially the idea of all those shade trees, which would keep ener-

41

gy use low in summer. And if the ice cream parlor is to be an all-electric building, the company will provide the first complement of light bulbs. Of course, we'll give—"

"Look here!" Peanuts pounded on the table. "We've been at this almost two hours. Toxic waste! Light bulbs! Criminy!   And not one word has been said about price. Price! Price for prime commercial property. Let's talk turkey. You're not going to have any ice cream at all, if you don't purchase the land. Now stop pussy-footin'!" He stared straight at Mayor Mashburn, who said the city manager should address that.

"But before Fred speaks," the mayor said, looking sheepish, "I need to share what's in my heart. My mind is absolutely for the town green, no question, but my heart fears that if it fails, Cadillac could lose all the prestige it's gained by having the Cougars be the regional champs. We could become the laughing stock of the state."

"Mr. Mayor," Wynona cooed. "We are all Cougars fans."

Having unburdened himself, Mashburn nodded at the city manager. "Fred, are you ready?"

Fred Miller knocked the edges of a stack of pages on the table and cleared his throat. "I have consulted three commercial realtors, one in Cadillac, one in Woodward, and one in Clinton, cities of corresponding size and growth potential, and this property which amounts to 1.765 acres is worth, when you take the average of comparable sites, $1.3 million."

"Oh, no you don't!" shouted Peanuts rising to his feet. "I'm not going to let you rob me. We're talking two full city blocks here. If I'd sell this for townhouses around the perimeter, I could easily make over eleven million."

"Not zoned residential." Fred Miller answered tersely.

"Maybe not yet, you idiot."

"No market for townhouses in Cadillac," Miller said without passion. "Everyone wants a yard. Plenty of land away from downtown."

Peanuts sputtered. "You all—You all have your boy primed to steal my land, and it's not going to happen."

"This is fair market value," said the city manager.

"I will never sell for any piddling $1.3 million."

"That's our offer," said the manager.

"To hell with you!" shouted Peanuts and pushed back his chair and headed for the door. His hand on the doorknob, he turned to yell at Wynona. "And don't try to condemn my buildings. If you demolish them I will just store more toilets, or maybe let that guy with the Porta-potties drain them right there on Main Street. You have ganged up on me, and you will be sorry!" He opened the door.

"Wait, Mr. Murphy!" Wynona Blosser called. "We need you to make this work."

Peanuts acted upon a lifelong urge by throwing Wynona Blosser the finger and was gone.

Interviews in *The Courier* revealed that the town had quickly splintered. Wynona's vision had captured the garden club, Rose Rock Country Club, the socially ambitious who looked to her as the gatekeeper, and many others who cared about the way Cadillac looked to visiting relatives and friends.

The words toxic waste had lit up the brains of those with pretensions to environmental concerns and those sincerely concerned about the purity of ground water. Lit up in equal numbers were the brains of those who resented the judgmental, busybody voices of the tree-huggers.

Also quite vocal were those who resented the lawyers, bankers, managers, engineers, and especially the hoity-toity members of the garden club who had the leisure to tell others what their true esthetic needs were.

Also in the local paper was evidence of a majority who did not know or care what the latest fuss was about. They get home from work tired and struggle to put a meal on the table while pushing their children to do homework.

But of all the citizens of Cadillac not one, with the possible exception of R.J. Bagby, gave any sympathy to Peanuts Murphy. And Peanuts felt this. While he drank and collected his rents, he nursed a growing hatred for the town on whose high school football team he had played valiantly, his hometown in every sense of the word, the town which now was trying to rob him. And he talked endlessly of this to any person who had the misfortune to pause in his vicinity. But he refused to speak to anyone attempting to reopen a discussion about a price for his property. "They will never get that land! No matter how much they offer," he told everyone in town.

The word pariah was whispered in city government circles, but still everyone was shocked when, less than a month after the meeting at the Chamber of Commerce Building, Peanuts' body was found at the bottom of a ravine.

That night, as the news of Peanuts Murphy's grisly death swirled through the town, Wynona's mind fled to the town green in Concord, Massachusetts. Louisa May Alcott, Henry David Thoreau, Nathaniel Hawthorne had lived in Concord. Wynona herself had been an English teacher. She belonged there where everything was leafy and literary, moist and mossy. She had visited the authors' graves and identified in herself a feeling of kinship.

Though she never got back East, through the years she fed her visions of a town green for Cadillac, and after seeing the movie, The Music Man, she added a bandstand to the picture. Her bank was going to provide the financing, and more important, it was her good taste that would guide the whole project. She had already found the little marble-top tables and the twisted wrought iron "ice cream" chairs in a catalog.

But now things could not have turned out worse, and she couldn't sleep. That tranquil green would have allowed her to be a better, more beautiful person, a woman who read more books and recalled what she'd learned in college and contemplated all this sitting under shade trees. That vision had been making her desperate for this project to succeed, but now, what happened to Peanuts was keeping her awake at night.

Mr. Murphy's body had been found near dusk by a hiker. In the light of morning the deputy found above the ravine tire tracks from what was later determined to be Peanuts' car, but the car, its nose severely dented and its side scraped, was found in Peanuts' driveway at home.

The Courier reporter, Hillary O'Brian, a hard-working divorced mother, camped out at the sheriff's office and tried to wheedle information. Sheriff Jake Hale, a serious, reticent man, told the reporter, "The body bore many scrapes and bruises typical of a man who had rolled down into a fifty-foot gorge. I've sent the body to the M.E. for the forensics." He said nothing else although he himself had been waylaid last week by Peanuts, who wanted the sheriff to look into a conspiracy against him.

Just in case Forensics reported evidence of a crime, Jake began quietly to interview each of the people who had been at that meeting in the Chamber of Commerce building, all of whom reported being insulted by Peanuts. The mayor reported a ferocious battle—"blood on the floor." But since neither a note-taker nor a recording device had been present at the meeting, Hale could put little faith in any of these reports.

His immediate plan was to find the next-of-kin, and on an anonymous tip from a female voice on the phone, he searched Peanuts' house and found a marriage certificate. Chub Widmer, the witness at the wedding, was dead, but the name of the bride on the somewhat tattered document was still clear: Victoria St. Buckingham. Seeing that the wedding had taken place in the Nightingale Chapel in Las Vegas, Hale was afraid this might be the made-up name of a stripper or some other person who frequently changed her name. But with the help of Las Vegas police, he was able to reach Victoria at home.

"I'd like to help you, Sheriff, but I'm probably the last person who could I.D. that guy. My sister told me I got married on the night you mentioned, but the guy ran off with the license, so I don't even know his name. I was only 17 and drunk as a skunk. That was over thirty years ago. I don't suppose he left me anything."

"Mr. Murphy didn't have a will as far as we've been able to find out."

"I was just joking. I didn't mean to be disrespectful."

"I've made inquiries, and there aren't any kin I've been able to find. Are you married to someone else?"

"No. I've dodged that bullet lots of times thanks to that one weird night. Every time a guy started to talk about moving in with me, I'd tell him I was married to a big businessman from Oklahoma. You meet so many jerks out here. I'm a grandmother. I've been working steadily at the Cheesecake House for years."

"Could you come and sign the papers? I'll get someone here to identify the body. It's in pretty bad shape."

"I'd like to help you, but a plane ticket—"

Never one to make promises casually, Hale said, "Can I call you back?"

The sheriff asked R.J., Peanuts' only pal, to identify the body. "Sure, I'll do it." They rode together in the hearse to Oklahoma City to retrieve the corpse.

The coroner's report was inconclusive. Multiple bruises and a compound skull fracture.

"Was he pushed? Did someone beat him to death?" Jake asked.

The coroner squinted through thick, smeared glasses. "Hard to tell," he said.

"Huh?"

"We didn't find a bullet, if that's what you're after. This isn't television. If a guy gets pushed, he gets pushed. There aren't going to be any marks from that."

"Well, could you tell me if he just rolled over the side of the ravine or if he dropped off the railroad trestle? Fifty feet."

"No. He wasn't dropped fifty feet. His skeleton is pretty much intact. It's just his hide that's ripped up. What killed him was landing on his head right off. There's no dirt under his fingernails like he tried to stop himself. He probably hit his head and broke his neck at the same time. If anyone cares, tell them he didn't suffer. Sign here," the coroner said, "and pick him up at the loading dock."

After buying some burgers and slushies, Jake and R.J. got on the road. "So, what do you think?" Jake asked casually as they ate in the car.

"Peanuts was always a crazy guy," R.J. said, chewing slowly. "I used to tell him he was a case of arrested development. But he got real obnoxious there at the end."

"Yeah?"

"He'd call me all times of the night and jaw on."

"Yeah?" Jake stuck with his usual monosyllabic interviewing technique.

"He told me that Blosser woman was plotting against him, maybe going to get him declared incompetent then grab his money. He said the whole sale and development thing would have gone his way if it weren't for her. Although other times he said she was for it, and it was the mayor who queered the deal. Sometimes he blamed the city manager."

"Oh?"

"He thought someone was following him. Maybe shooting video trying to catch him drunk. He said he had a witness who saw a guy with a camera."

"Who?"

"He didn't say. Said he felt like blowing up the bank, and asked me if I wanted to help him."

"What'd you say?"

"I didn't have to say anything 'cause he just went right on raving about how he was going to sell all his other property and put all the money into gold. After he bought the dynamite for the bank, that is." R.J. took another bite.

"You believe any of that about the Blosser woman?"

"Nope. I just wanted to get off the phone."

At home, alone, in his house between the parking lots of the Krispy Kreme and K-Mart, Jake sat down and turned on the local ten o'clock news in time to see the mayor saying, "This murderer must be caught before he strikes again." Jake stood and stretched. What evidence did he have? From R.J.'s report it sounded like Peanuts was having delusions. But there still could have been a crime. Paranoids had enemies too.

In the Busy Bee Café the collection for the plane ticket took about three minutes. Everyone wanted to get in on helping the widow from Las Vegas, including Sloane Willard who dropped in a twenty. The deputy, Fred, had gotten on the internet and found a good deal on a flight.

Jake felt better knowing that a person connected to a legal document, albeit a Vegas marriage license, was on her way. She would be able to get some money out of the bank to bury Peanuts and take care of any other arrangements.

"This is weird," Victoria said on the drive back from the airport. "I don't even know the guy, and here I am playing his wife."

"You are his wife. His widow actually," Jake said. He was relieved to see that Victoria St. Buckingham was an ordinary-looking woman. She was tall and carried her middle-age weight well. He could tell she was still proud of her body, but he could also imagine her as a lean 17-year-old bent on adventure. Had she bluffed her way into casinos where she met bumpkins like Peanuts? Had he flashed a lot of cash, maybe bought her a diamond ring or a fur coat or whatever the greedy-all-night merchants on the strip had to offer people drunk on the belief that no one at home would ever know.

"Have any trouble getting here?" Jake asked.

"No. My sister helped me, loaned me clothes and took me to the airport."

Besides some colorful boots, she was dressed in slacks and a nice V-neck sweater, clothes like the average Cadillac housewife wore to church. Her long auburn hair was pulled back with a horseshoe-shaped barrette. She had a throaty voice, and he wondered if she'd ever been a singer.

51

"So, you've lived in Las Vegas all your life?"

"No. My people are from Georgia. My sister and I ran away when she was nineteen and I was sixteen. I wouldn't have stayed in Las Vegas except that she married a croupier and had three kids, and they and my son are the only family I've got." She glanced at Jake before going on. "Things were so bad when we first got to Vegas, no jobs, everyone trying to take advantage of us, especially her — totally gorgeous. We made beds and washed toilets for the first year." Victoria paused and looked out at the fence posts whizzing past.

"My sister told me that the night before Peanuts and me got married I'd come to her and said, 'I've met a rich guy and he's going to take care of me back in Oklahoma.' She cried and said don't go, but she said I just ignored her and went off to The Tropicana, a place I'd never dreamed I'd get inside. I wish I could remember it. Two days later I woke up at home with a gold ring on my finger. She said when he brought me back to our place, both him and me were crying."

No one wanted to speak ill of the dead. The people who had known Peanuts were so relieved he was gone they felt guilty. As Victoria was introduced around town, an image began to take shape of a Stanley Woolmont Murphy, (no one had known his full name until the obituary ran in *The Courier*), a wonderful man full of civic pride. "Hail fellow well met," old Donavan, the funeral director, said to Victoria. "Years ago he built a pool hall so the young would have a place to go after school," the minister reported. "Good old Peanuts," many said.

Victoria teared up hearing the praise from her erstwhile husband's townspeople, and this moved several of the women to offer her a place to stay and a tour of the town. Only Wynona Blosser steered clear of Victoria St. Buckingham, and a few people remarked on how uncharacteristic of Wynona this was, not to be at the center of things.

After the funeral and while the Faithful Elders Sunday School Class served coffee and donuts in the Baptist church basement, Wynona Blosser found herself standing along the wall next to Victoria St. Buckingham.

"Hi," Wynona said when Victoria caught her staring. The widow looked low class, from that drugstore dye job right down to her cheap high heels.

"Hi." Victoria lowered her eyes.

"I'm Wynona."

"I'm Vicki."

And then silence set in. Wynona wanted to make an excuse and move away, but that seemed rude. And there was something easygoing about this woman from Las Vegas. "That's a nice dress." Wynona said.

"Thanks. My sister and I call it our church lady

dress." Victoria's voice, low and wise-sounding, and her bald honesty caused Wynona to ask, "Would you like to go get a drink after this?"

"When will it be over?"

"It can be over right now if you want. Just go over to that elderly woman, Margaret Bailey, the one with the white hair. See her there. Tell her how much you appreciate all she and the other ladies have done, and how proud Peanuts would be to have his Faithful Elders Sunday School Class turn out for him like this. Then go over to the minister and thank him for the beautiful service. I'll be out front in a black Mercedes."

Victoria put herself on autopilot as she did when she was at work. She spoke the Wynona words to Margaret Bailey and then to the preacher. They worked like a charm. The preacher seemed to welcome the idea that the party was over.

Victoria let her head drop back on the leather headrest of Wynona's Mercedes. "Thank you. Thank you."

Wynona had pulled out of the church parking lot in the direction of Antoine's intending to show Victoria what a classy bar Cadillac had, but halfway there she made a swooping U-turn. "Let's go to my house." This felt like the right move although she hadn't opened her home to anyone new in decades.

Since her husband's death six months ago, the house had changed. It was still its big old frumpy yellow brick self, but it felt cozier now. She'd eliminated the cigar stench when she threw out all the carpets, all the drapes, and all his clothes.

The rooms themselves softened and enclosed her in a sweet-smelling embrace. She was alone, but at least there was no one there to make her feel misunderstood. Old Floyd had never denied her anything, but he treated her ideas as silly whims to be indulged because he had the money to do it. She felt more herself tonight than she had since her marriage.

"What'll you have?" Wynona asked as she and Victoria walked into what Wynona called her boudoir—a second story sitting room attached to her bedroom, a place to entertain one's closest friends. She seated Victoria in the downy lap of an overstuffed yellow-flowered chair with a large, matching footstool. After handing Victoria her bourbon and taking a swig of her own, Wynona sat down in a matching chair and put her feet up on the footstool beside Victoria's.

Victoria, who had been off-balance since coming to Cadillac, began to relax after her second drink. She was far from home. She'd never been in a private home this grand, but sitting in the early evening shadows with a generous woman was deeply familiar. She and her sister had kept this ritual even when the kids were still at home. After the kids were in bed, the women would sit and sip their drinks and murmur to each other, or say nothing because everything had already been said between sisters. Then Victoria would go to work.

Wynona sipped slowly, wondering what they were going to talk about.

"It looks like you've had a wonderful life," Victoria said.

"I've been trying to get out of this town since I was a girl, but yes, comparatively speaking—" Wynona stopped herself and regretted what sounded like condescension.

"Sure, comparatively speaking," Victoria said.

"I'm, I'm sorry to—"

"Oh, hush. I'm not offended. Everything is comparative. I think about that all the time. When I'm down, I say, Victoria, at least you don't live in a leaky trailer. At least you aren't in some crummy women's prison. At least you have indoor plumbing." Victoria glanced at her hostess over her glass. "That last was a joke. I've always had indoor plumbing."

As Victoria drank more, her voice got lower, more dusky and beautiful to Wynona's ear. They sat quietly, two widows of men they didn't miss.

"Maybe you wonder about me." Victoria said. "You know, a gal from Sin City."

"Oh no, I mean there are a lot of honest jobs in Las Vegas."

"Yeah, but they don't pay as well."

Wynona felt a prickle of heat on her arms. "Jake said

you worked in a bakery."

"The Cheesecake House is no bakery. Of course the traffic's way down for a woman my age. I live with my sister's family." Victoria sounded relaxed and her Georgia drawl was growing thicker.

Victoria felt relieved to have come clean with her hostess, and Wynona struggled to adjust to the level of candor that now pervaded her boudoir. Finally she sighed with the realization that what she'd wanted tonight was a stranger to talk to. "I ought to tell you how Peanuts died," she said.

"What? You know what happened?"

"Yeah. I know." Wynona was immediately sorry she'd started this.

"So, what happened?

"I should tell the sheriff, but I feel like it's too late."

"Go on, tell me."

"You don't know how scared I am."

"What have you got to be scared of?"

Wynona felt her eyes sting.

"Don't be afraid. Just tell me what happened to Peanuts?"

Wynona paused to prepare her thoughts. It was almost dark in the room. She began very quietly. "Peanuts wanted to sell his property in the middle of town. The city offered him a price he didn't like. I had told the mayor it was too low and would insult Peanuts, but he thought we ought to start low, and the city manager said his figures couldn't justify starting any higher. They both are scared to death of being accused of squandering the people's money, so the offer was made in a flat out way. Nothing to invite a counter offer. I don't know how that meeting got so out of hand, but Peanuts left very angry, and the upshot was that he wouldn't even consider talking to us again. He felt he'd been disrespected and was going to make us sorry by not selling at all.

"I'll be honest with you, Vicki, I wanted the city to have that land like I've never wanted anything else. I didn't care how we got it or what we had to pay. I wanted Cadillac to have a beautiful center, a park, something for everyone, something we could be proud of."

"So?"

"So he wouldn't deal with anybody. But I felt that if anyone could change his mind or at least his mood, it was me. He didn't like me, but I knew that I was the one person he would believe if I told him we'd pay four million. And sometimes a woman can put things gently and turn a man around. You know what I mean?"

"Sure."

"Here's what happened. I was downtown late helping Floyd Jr. go over loan applications. He'd gotten so behind I was embarrassed to face people. It was nearly midnight then, and he was pooped, so I told him to go on. Later, as I was finishing up, I looked down from the window and saw Peanuts on the side street haranguing a couple of guys. I ran to open the safe and took out $50,000, which I stuck way in the bottom of my big leather bag. I got to the sidewalk in time to see Peanuts, totally smashed, getting into his car. I rapped on the passenger-side window and asked if I could speak to him for a minute. He wouldn't even roll down the window, just began to swear at me. He was frantically trying to get the key in the ignition, and I swung open the door and jumped in. Where I got the nerve I don't know. I felt desperate, like getting him to sell was all I'd ever wanted. He hit the gas and we roared down Main, side-swiping a small pickup on our way, Peanuts cussing up a storm and yelling at me to get out of his car, but he was going so fast—if I'd jumped, it would have killed me.

"'Listen to me!' I screamed. 'That fool city manager insulted you. I apologize. Look at what I have for you. It's in your interest.' Of course, he was yelling too, so I don't think he heard much. He was blind drunk, barely staying on the road, much less in his lane. We were out east of town by then on a country road. What would people have thought if we'd both died in that old Impala? Me and Peanuts running away with $50,000 of the bank's money?"

"I see what you mean."

"I was going to give it to him as earnest money, but when I started rummaging in my bag for the cash, he saw this, swerved, and we hit a tree. He lurched out of the car yelling, "Don't kill me," and ran down a slope and then over the edge of the gorge. I heard a scream, then nothing but rocks thumping and bushes tearing away."

The room was quiet except for two women breathing.

"God," Victoria whispered. "What'd you do with the car?"

"I drove it back to town, parked it in his driveway and walked home. Even though it was the middle of the night, there must have been someone who saw me. It'll be a miracle if no one turns me in."

"But it was an accident. That's all." Victoria let out a little sigh. "That's all, Wynona."

Wynona leaned her head back on the chair and let the tears run into her hair. This is what she'd been blindly headed for when she invited Victoria home: understanding. They were quiet together for a while until Victoria raised up to face Wynona.

"Sorry to say it, but I think you need to tell this to the sheriff. He's a good guy and has seriously tried to find out what happened."

"I don't know if I can. I didn't check on the body. I've withheld evidence. About a death."

The next morning Victoria and Wynona entered the sheriff's office accompanied by Tim Ragan, the best defense lawyer in Oklahoma, who had flown his own plane into the Cadillac airstrip at dawn.

After giving her statement, Wynona called Hillary O'Brian at *The Courier* and told her she would come in as soon as she got back from the airport. Jake made no promises or even predictions about what the penalties would be and called the judge, who said he would schedule a hearing.

Wynona felt strangely passive. Normally so hard-driving, she was glad to let events take their course. Her dream of a town green for Cadillac was going to be realized; Victoria had agreed to sell for $3,000,000 and this buoyed Wynona enormously. What felt equally and strangely inspiring was that her own role in the town was bound to change. The monolith of the banker's wife would crack now that she would be seen as a woman who took a desperate risk by confessing.

After leaving the sheriff's office, Wynona drove Victoria to the bank to withdraw the contents of all three of Peanuts' accounts, $859,743. Victoria deposited half in a new account in her own name. And half she stuck in her purse in the form of a cashier's check. With Tim Ragan's help they drew up a contract for the sale of the land. Then Wynona drove Victoria to the airport. Ragan took off in his own plane.

At the gate Wynona hugged Victoria and said, "Make sure the broker you get is on the level. We'll talk more about our project after you get home. You should stay with me for the groundbreaking."

Wynona watched Victoria disappear into the security line, then stood at a window and waited for the plane to take off. Nothing would be the same now. Some of the people of Cadillac might sympathize with her. The majority would either laugh at the banker's widow for getting in a car with a drunk, or would want to put her in the state hospital, but she knew the truth, and the truth was she'd jumped into that old Impala for love of beauty.

§

THE COURIER REPORTER
2013

From Hillary O'Brian's point of view *The Courier* offices reeked of men. Not just decades of their sweating deadlines. The Essence of Courier, as she called it, was mostly due to the ever-present cigar smoke that seeped from under the editor's door and had soaked into the floors, woodwork, and obsolete furniture. The editor's own office, cluttered and dusty, was more unpleasant than the outer office space where she worked with Duffy, a nice old hack. Mr. Tarman, the editor, had been limited by the Board of Health to smoking his stogies at his desk behind a closed door. The big glass windows looking onto the office were so coated with smoke that, as Hillary observed, "It's eternal evening in there."

Hillary instinctively inhaled before entering. "Mr. Tarman, you said you wanted to see me."

"Yeah," Tarman said and shuffled the newspapers, memos, and empty coffee cups searching for something on his desk. "This town green story has blown up now that there's been a death, and I'm giving it to Duffy."

"But this is my story."

"Look, lady, it was a story about a big city garden when I put you on it. Now we've got a banker who has confessed to concealing evidence."

"That's right. Wynona Blosser called me just before she put the widow on the plane back to Las Vegas."

"She called you?"

"Yep. She said we would talk more as her case progressed."

"Wynona Blosser called you?"

"This is my story, Mr. Tarman, and it's just going to get bigger. The dates for the cleanup and groundbreaking haven't even been set. Judianne McCall, the wife of the mayor's lawyer, told me that at the meeting last week to finalize the sale of Murphy's land, there was talk of testing the soil for toxicity, but when I asked the city engineer if they were going to do it, he said it had been agreed at the meeting that it wasn't necessary."

Tarman shifted his cigar to the front of his face where his brown teeth clenched it for hissing inhales. "Well." But before he could go on, he erupted in deep, bulky, wet coughs. "We'll see how it goes," he wheezed.

Hillary also was coughing, but she stopped long enough to say, "I want my own column."

"Don't get ahead of yourself. I never gave Duffy a column. You two are the reporters."

Hillary went back to her desk and automatically opened her laptop, but she put her hands in her lap. She was proud that she'd held onto her story, but she needed this job to grow. It was part of her survival plan.

The Cadillac Courier was the only newspaper

in a booming town with a community college, which had been covered only once since she'd arrived at this job three months ago, and that was Duffy's story about a student who rammed his motorcycle into a hedge of rosebushes and strangle vine, having to be extricated by firemen. No articles on new professors. No articles on the college's mission or funding. Furthermore, there was the Juvenile Detention Center on the edge of town, everyone pretended didn't exist. It must be bursting with stories. The merchants and restaurants never got feature pieces. City government was Tarman's sole focus, especially when it impacted the schools or sewer system.

"Duffy," Hillary said. The other reporter raised his shaggy head and smiled. "What do you know about circulation?"

"Mr. Tarman keeps track of that."

"But what are the numbers? Is the paper's readership expanding or shrinking?"

Duffy shrugged. "He keeps all that to himself."

"Can I ask him what it is?"

"Oh gosh." Duffy's eyes widened behind the thick lenses of his glasses. "I wouldn't do that. I mean, really. He wouldn't like that."

"Really. Hmm."

"You're new here," he said.

"Would R.J. know about circulation? Of course he would. He sells the advertising. He'd have to know." R.J.

was almost as new as she was, also in his thirties. His job here was very part time. He supported himself with odd construction jobs and could be seen hanging out at the Busy Bee Café. He was the right kind of handsome, easygoing guy to sell a few ads for the paper.

Hillary closed her laptop, grabbed her bag and headed out to find R.J. Bagby. He was there with Floyd Blosser, the banker's son, sitting at the table in the Busy Bee's front window.

"Hi, guys, what's for breakfast?"

"R.J.'s going to take me fishing down on Fuller Creek," Floyd said.

"Ah," Hillary said. "What are you using for bait?"

"I already bought the worms." Floyd started to reach under the table to show her.

"That's all right, Floyd. I just wanted to ask R.J. what the circulation is at *The Courier*."

R.J. grinned. "Beats me. Tarman asked me to sell ads. Merchants know *The Courier* is on its last legs. They wouldn't embarrass me by asking about circulation. The big outfits like Bob's Furniture and Farley's Hardware do television."

"Thanks, R.J. Good to see you, Floyd. I'll let you guys get on down to the creek."

Hillary walked to the car in the glaring sunshine. Last legs? Her job at the paper had been her long-term plan. Her heart was beating hard. She'd been so furious and bull-headed-proud at the time of the divorce that she'd given up too much to her ex. She had to have this job.

She got in her Civic and turned on the air conditioning. Tarman was shortsighted in his vision for the paper. Why was he letting it drift into the ditch? That would be a big story: Editor Kills His Own Paper.

She didn't really know his story except that he had been divorced in the late 80s. She wasn't dumb enough to push him on the circulation numbers. But if *The Courier* really went under, she and poor old Duffy would be out on the street.

Being a divorced mother living outside of town, Hillary's personal life was now contained in a small orbit: care for her ten-year-old daughter, maintain a small farmhouse, and go to work. When she was married, she and Robert had a social life with other couples. But now, any activities outside the home were planned to the taste of a ten-year-old. At least her evenings were available to write up her stories. And with no husband to talk to, she was free to scheme about her still-modest career.

The next morning she entered the gummy interior of Mr. Tarman's nicotine den. "I have a proposition for you, Mr. Tarman."

He looked surprised. She hadn't knocked.

"I believe my idea for a column will raise the number of subscriptions. We both know that number is inching down. If, after my column has run for six weeks, that downward trend has ceased, I get to keep going."

"Hold on now."

"It wouldn't be my writing."

"What?"

"It would be an opportunity for your readers to send in—"

"We've got an advice column already. Dear Amy. A chance for readers to lay out the pathetic details of their love lives."

"No, this is a chance to express themselves about their town. 'Cadillac Voices.' This would give readers a bit of a stake in the paper. They could contribute pieces of local history. Information that only they have because it's been passed down in their family."

Tarman leaned back and chewed on his cigar. "You know what you're going to get—a lot of illiterate yammering, and then we'll have to discontinue the column and a few readers will be pissed and cancel their subscriptions."

Tarman sat up straighter. "I started this paper over forty years ago. It was going to inform opinions, get people talking about local and state issues, raise the level of conversation!" His nostrils flared and he stared straight ahead. "Oh, it was going to be a big asset to the community until everybody got their news from television and then everybody got their news from computers. Besides, you don't want to know what's out there. A lot of empty-headed, knee-jerk spewing that people will pass off as their opinions. I know this town, kiddo."

"But we have experts here. People over at the community college. There are more PhDs over there than you'd think. This could tap into what they have to offer. Believe me. If they wrote it, they will want to read it and have their colleagues read it. They'll put it on their resumés, for godsake."

"You'll have to insist on a word limit if you get those people involved."

"Let's try it. What have we got to lose? People will be proud to see their piece in their hometown paper."

"And fix all the spelling and grammar in the rest. Maybe some old-timers could give us some history we could use as filler."

"What could be great is hearing from young people about their jobs or students talking about their classes. Newcomers, what are their first impressions? Are we as friendly a town as our advertising says we are?"

Tarman hissed a long sigh. "I'm warning you, this is going bring in a load of crap."

"Okay. We'll see. I'll write a short piece announcing it." She smiled.

"Hold on now. We'll see if we get anything the first time."

Three weeks later Hillary had made her selection for the first Voice. She threw a headline on it and carried it into Mr. Tarman's office.

WHEN IT WAS REALLY DRY

People in Cadillac keep complaining about the weather. This ain't dry, what you see here today. When an old-time Oklahoman says things were dry, he is talking about saplings keeling over and blowing away, the hot night wind sweeping away the earth around the hair-like roots of your hand-watered tomato plants, and the earth cracking open. The young don't know about the old days when the dead grass could cut your bare feet.

As a kid I remember watching a river of red Jello melt into the pool of oleo on my supper plate. The heat was still there at bedtime and no air conditioning. Mama would sponge us off and salt us with talcum powder, which would turn to pasty rings around our sweaty little necks. Heat stayed all night, so the adults in the family would give up on sleep and sit on the screened porch murmuring to each other through the night about the 1930's droughts when farmers were forced to feed milk cows on Russian thistles and soapweed, when a cloud of grasshoppers came down to eat the young wheat, followed by a plague of black widow spiders and marauding rabbits. I heard them say the Agriculture Department in Washington told men to pile the dust back on their fields to hold the moisture. I heard them say women used a cup of water to wash a whole day's dishes.

George Huston
Cadillac resident since 1951

Mr. Tarman stared at the essay long after he'd had time to read it. "Who's this George Huston?"

"I don't know. What do you think?"

"Do you think he made it up about the spiders and the rabbits?"

"I checked with the University Archives down in Norman. It's all true."

"We forget so much," Tarman sighed and rested his cigar on the edge of his desk. "I mean as a people. We forget what our grandfathers —"

"Your folks were pioneers?"

"People now think it's romantic!" Mr. Tarman's usually impassive face twisted. "Romantic — that dugout living, eating possum, all those hungry, barefoot years, attending a one-room schoolhouse. Oh, how wonderful they were, everybody says — ignorant, plain ignorant of what life could be like under a tyrant of a schoolmaster whose cane went unchallenged by anyone."

"But you weren't alive back then."

"The 30s were what hardened my parents, who nearly starved in the Oklahoma Panhandle—gaunt-eyed, sway-backed, ragged children of bull-headed parents holding onto the worthless claim they'd inherited. Desperate children who grew up to be tyrants themselves." Tarman's eyes flashed, angry, indignant. "People forget, dammit, what this guy is talking about." The editor thumped hard on the sheet of paper on his desk. "Everybody wants to believe a hard life builds character. Sometimes it just makes you mean. People talk like Oklahoma history was all one big rodeo, bootstraps, Wild Bill Hickok stealing the charter from Guthrie, riding hell-for-leather, making Oklahoma City the Capitol. That's us, the Sooner State, thieves and cheaters and—" He cut himself off and looked at Hillary as though she'd suddenly appeared. He stared back down at the piece she'd handed him. "You're not going to get another one like this," he murmured.

"No, of course not. Who knows what's out there."

After six weeks of publishing a weekly Voice, Hillary asked Mr. Tarman about the circulation.

He frowned. "Had some calls from new subscribers."

"But we need a number, a baseline from which to keep up with what's working and what isn't."

His frown deepened. "No one's cancelled."

"No one has cancelled in six weeks? Is that unusual?"

Tarman looked with pained eyes at the ceiling. He was softly panting through parted lips. This newspaper, perhaps all he had in his nicotine-stained life, had been dying. Hillary realized he probably hadn't let himself check on the circulation count in a long time. He couldn't have given her a number. His face darkened, straining, aching not to show emotion over the possible revival of his youthful dream.

§

Judianne McCall was 432 pages into *Moby Dick* when she stopped to rest her neck—nearly 35 years old and just now reading what she should have been given in high school. Mrs. Peevy at the library had looked at her through goggle-thick lenses to say, "Reading Melville will teach you about the American mind." Judianne took that as a promise, and she had to admit when she had this big heavy book open on the screened-in porch, her tattered little dictionary close at hand, she felt smarter. And not so lonely. *Moby Dick*, all about water and whales and boats, was a real stretch for an Oklahoma girl in 2011.

Gavin came home around 9:00 p.m. She was shredding potatoes at the kitchen counter. This kitchen, in what would soon be called their old house, was shined up in that sweet, storybook way she'd loved when they first got married—a sampler with their names in a heart, a row of canisters with darling little girls painted on them, the daisy wallpaper. She felt more at home here than she'd ever feel in that stainless steel bowling alley the architect called a kitchen.

Gavin dropped his sport coat on a chair and scratched his formerly perfect belly. At times like this,

his blond hair hanging in his eyes, his grin gone a little loopy, he was just a simple creature waiting to be fed. And she was just the girl to do it. "Hungry?" she asked.

He slid his fingers under the hair at the back of her neck and lifted the red curls. His whiskey breath against her neck arrived with a kiss so tender she wasn't sure his lips had touched. The shiver stiffened her titties on the way down. Gavin had what Grandma called "the touch," and Judianne had married him for that, though, naturally, everybody thought it was the money. She turned and took his hand to kiss his palm. Yep, an expensive perfume on his fingers. The florist. A flash of heat made her eyes sting. She swallowed.

"Sometimes," she began in a dreamy voice, "I think about not being here at all when you come home."

The hand which had lifted the hair now gently cupped the back of her neck, fingers and thumb pressing. "I sure would miss my little redneck," he whispered in her ear. "Have to call out the dogs. Right?"

"Right," she twisted away and inhaled.

"If I don't eat something soon—" he said.

"These here are ready to go." She dumped the potatoes in the hot Crisco, where they squawked and gobbled. "Did ya have a nice day?"

He leaned against the edge of the counter top and folded his arms. "Yeah, Judith, you know how I love the law." If his daddy hadn't sent over something more exciting, he'd probably spent the day making out wills. He hated other people's wills. She shook the skillet. Her name never had been Judith.

"You know, hon," she said and arranged his potatoes on a platter to keep warm in the oven, "I can't help but say it one more time. You could make a killing on that new place once it's finished."

He didn't say anything, just shook his head, chin riding slowly from shoulder to shoulder. She set a plate, knife and fork, a glass of beer, and a bottle of A-1 sauce on the kitchen table. "We could sell it and then build that cabin we used to dream about up in Colorado on the side of a mountain."

He sat down. "Look, kid, Cadillac is our town. Anywhere else we'd be outsiders, people with no influence. We've talked about this."

She ran the hot water hard, letting the whoosh and the steam rise around her face as she stared into the skillet. She always liked something to be humming when he was home, the radio or the air conditioner, some kind of sound to float her mind on. She'd been up to the site of the new house—so many glass walls staring her own self back at her—curly red hair flying around the face of a skinny little woman in blue jeans and T-shirt who looked real straight for someone who felt kinda bent. "You are the cutest little thing I ever saw," Gavin always said whenever she asked why he married her. "And I'm gonna give you the world." But it wasn't going to be the world. It was going to be Cadillac—the most stuck-up town in Oklahoma.

Suddenly, aware Gavin had said something, she looked up. On the counter the raw steak lay on the red-soaked meat paper, the juice running onto the floor. She scooped up the steak and held it limp across her palm. "A what?" she asked.

"A housewarming. The boys are almost finished with the interior. We can move in another few weeks. We ought to have a great big party. Champagne, the works. You get the food lined up, and I'll take care of making sure the yard looks good. And we're gonna need all new furniture for the downstairs."

"Our house ain't no country club." She rubbed the blood off the floor with paper towel.

"Come on, everybody in town is dying to get inside and see the twenty-foot ceiling in the living room and go up top to look through my telescope at the stars. There's nothing like it anywhere around. Real architectural design—volcanic rock, glass and redwood. The fire marshal told me he can smell the resin from Main Street."

She dropped the steak on the broiler pan, so hot it cracked like a bullet. One of his women gave him this housewarming idea, another plan to show Judianne up as a hick. Who could like a town where the health of children didn't figure in city planning. Where absolutely everybody either belonged to the country club or wished they did. And it wasn't really a club, like friends having fun. Even the women, dressed up and smelling sweet, faced off at each other in the ladies' room like sluts at some honky-tonk. Janet Fullenweider, who knew very well Judianne had cleaned for Gavin's mother when she was in high school, pulled her lips over her big teeth to ask, "Judianne, honey, how'd you and Gavin ever meet?" What kind of town was this to raise a child in?

After she served the steak and potatoes, she poured herself a shot of whiskey and sat on the kitchen stool beside the counter, looking down at her bare toes. "Gavin? Don't you think it's time I stopped taking the pill?"

"Where'd you buy this steak?"

"Is it tough?"

"It sure as hell is."

She sipped her whiskey. Did Gavin understand the American mind? He was the smartest man she'd ever met, a lawyer. He said he'd read *Moby Dick* in high school, but he'd never sit still that long for anybody else's ideas.

He finished every scrap of food on his plate and reached into the kitchen drawer for the measuring tape and drafting pad. As she watched, he began to measure the height of his lap from the floor. He jotted notes for the architect. "You know, Jude, this desk has got to be one and three-quarter inches higher than standard."

"Really?"

He stretched out his arm and held one end of the measuring tape in his teeth. "What do you think," he asked pointing to one of his drawings, "these shelves at my eye level?"

"Gonna have the chair contoured to fit your balls, Gavin?"

He gave her a sidelong glare. "What's wrong with you tonight?"

What was wrong with her, she decided as she stared at the bedroom ceiling, was that something was leaking into her brain. Something dark and oozy like a slug dragging a shiny track of dread across her thoughts, making her feel she ought to speak up before it was too late. But she didn't know what to do, so she just made trouble for herself, like tonight.

Seated on the screened-in porch, she laid her pen on the little metal table and studied the thirty-seventh invitation she'd written today. Cadillac was a big town, not fancy, just spread out, especially now that the county had expanded the orphanage into a children's prison out on the highway and the community college was getting bigger and hiring real professors. She rubbed her neck. Writing these things out by hand was a whole lot easier than ordering them printed from Mr. Helander, who'd look over his glasses like she didn't even know how to spell. Ishmael, the boy telling the story in *Moby Dick*, said he'd rather be friends with Queequeg, the ignorant, pagan harpooner than with Christians who offered nothing but "hollow courtesy."

She looked at one of the invitations, the furls and curlicues of her elegant script, the only nice thing her grandmother had to pass on to her. She pressed the stiff card to her heart. Grandmother Virginia, raised without a father on a dried up farm in the '30s, rest her soul, told her to find a friend to marry. How was it people decided the way they were going to be married? Gavin's parents sure didn't act like friends. They just slid along on top of life, as though they were moving across crusted snow, never breaking through. Mr. McCall let his wife spend money like water. Mrs. McCall laughed off his mean remarks. They bought new stuff when they were bored, traveled separately when they were angry. Dodging and weaving. It worked. Nobody in town saw anything over at their house but a real sweet couple.

She picked up her pen. What she wanted to do was read *Moby Dick*. She'd left the crew of the Pequod in a terrible fix—an awful storm coming up and some mysterious aliens on board. But she needed to work on the party. Luckily, Gavin's mother had made her a list.

She'd let Gavin tell her they couldn't have a baby until he'd finished law school, passed the bar, established himself as a lawyer, and they had a bigger house. And they couldn't move to Colorado during the lifetime of his grandfather, an old man Gavin never visited. After the grandfather died, Gavin started building the new house. As she darted from her car to the bakery, the liquor store, and the farm supply for kerosene for the torches, she imagined herself building a big bonfire. She'd soak all Gavin's fancy suits with kerosene and use them as kindling. All that redwood, hundreds of yards of drapes. It'd go up with a terrific whump.

And yet, damn, this morning he'd wiped away all her nervousness about the party. "Poor little redneck. Don't you know whatever way we do this housewarming will be the way everybody will do things in Cadillac after this." She hadn't cared what he was saying because he held her as gently as a bird, rocking. She would never give this up. Her own marriage, like the whale, was what Melville would call inscrutable.

The new dining table was being built in Tulsa. Gavin sent a truck to pick it up. Even though she'd never been in an expensive furniture store, he made her go alone to Landsaw's. After they got married, she'd furnished their whole house with hand-me-downs from Mrs. McCall. Last night she'd drawn a picture of the new living room on a piece of notebook paper, but that didn't make her feel any better.

Mr. Landsaw himself grabbed his clipboard and rushed right up when he saw her come through the door. A small man with a tiny mustache, Mr. Landsaw lived with his wife next door to Gavin's parents. Judianne took a deep breath. "I need some living room furniture and some dining room chairs," she said, while her trembling fingers dug in her bag for the sketch.

"Of course, Mrs. McCall. Are you interested in Scandinavian, Mediterranean—"

"How about that couch over there?"

"That is the finest Italian leather, very contemporary. That particular shade of white is—"

"How about I just take three of those. Everybody should be able to sit around the fire."

"Just like the one there? Three? I don't—I can call the manufacturer, but—" His mustache twitched. Obviously this was not the way to furnish a home, but it was the only way she could get through it, like holding her nose and jumping into the deep end.

"And some big ole chairs, three or four, maybe like those in the corner, maybe four or five—I don't know. You mix and match."

He looked at her, his eyebrows tugged up painfully high on his forehead.

"Throw in some little tables to put drinks on, some lamps. What have you got for dining room chairs?"

She was out of there in twenty-five minutes, including all the paper work on the furniture as well as buying a copy of a real oil painting—a harpooner standing erect, being rowed across a stormy ocean. Delivery was arranged for a week before the party. She was still trembling when she got out onto the sidewalk. The florist was next.

"Why, Judianne, honey!" Marlys stood there in her sandals and striped apron, a little trowel in her hand, looking like someone on television about to tell you how easy it was to have a yard full of beautiful flowers. Marlys's shop was packed with plants—vines and blooming bushes, tall buckets of flowers behind the foggy refrigerator door, ferns and trees you could walk right under. A flagstone walkway curved between high banks of moist greenery.

"I need some flowers for a party. A dozen big bouquets, you mix and match." She turned to go.

"Oh honey, you can't get by with that. The floral arrangements for that house must be carefully designed. Like your fireplace wall," she continued. "All those little crevices in that volcanic rock should be planted with hanging vines. And the entry should have pots of blooming plants to guide the guests toward the living room."

It was clear Marlys had already been shown the house and had been dreaming up these arrangements like it was her own place. She'd love standing on a ladder getting all the vines dangling just right above Gavin McCall's living room. Is this what Gavin had in mind when he sent his wife to stand on this stone floor and tremble like a leaf?

"No," Judianne whispered.

"No?" Marlys replied, her eyes wide, her little pink mouth holding its O shape.

"No."

The August sun was blinding as it glanced off the cars parked at the strip mall. Now she had no flowers. They'd seemed the most important thing to Gavin's mother. "Don't skimp on the flowers," she'd said. Judianne stood in the hot wind with her legs apart like she was balancing on the deck of a ship and watched the dust kick up waves beside the highway. Nothing at the grocery store's chintzy floral department would do. This was the only florist in town—this town where every day she felt herself aging, her fertility drying up. After she turned thirty, she began to imagine her eggs toughening like the peel on oranges left out in a bowl for show. By now they were probably ash. She could stand to go on living here, but she would grow to hate Gavin if he wouldn't agree to having a baby.

She walked deliberately toward the car where the corner of the new oil painting peeked up from the back seat. She took hold of the hot door handle, got in and started driving. Onto that bonfire she would pile all that precious stuff out of the attic—Gavin's baby clothes, cub scout uniform and all the letters he wrote home from that fancy boys' camp in Michigan. She'd take the car's cigarette lighter to one of the torches along the driveway, then walk up holding it like a harpoon—a wild-haired woman reflected in a plate-glass window, resting her blazing torch on a redwood sill, drafts lifting her curly hair and tiny sparks dancing about it like Christmas lights. That silver baby cup with his adorable teeth marks would melt into a shiny little puddle.

About sixteen miles down the road she found another flower shop, not so fancy as Miss Striped Apron's, but the florist, a young man with bleached hair and tight jeans, was not likely to be Gavin's type. "I'd like us to totally design arrangements for my new house over in Cadillac— make the stone wall all viney. Two or three thousand dollar's worth. Can you handle that?"

He grinned. "Lady, you want vines? For two or three thousand dollars, me and you can be Tarzan and Jane."

Before the housewarming, she sat down on one of the new white couches to read. The light, the leather upholstery, everything felt alien in comparison to her spot on the screened-in porch at the old house. She missed the sultry air and the sounds of birds, but she'd get used to this in time. Very soon she came to the flash-quick ending of *Moby Dick*—such a long rambling book to cut her off so fast, everyone lost but Ishmael, who was rescued by a Captain searching for his own sons lost in the deep. She cried a little over the bigness of it all, then climbed up to the room Gavin called the observatory and looked out over Cadillac. There wasn't any mind more American than Gavin's. He called all the shots, not because he was so smart, but because he could. And he could because she let him. She stepped over to position her eye on the telescope, but what she saw was inscrutable. She took her eye away from the telescope to figure out what she was seeing. "Ha!" She'd been looking at Gavin down in the yard, his rump to be exact, as he bent over planting mums. The hip pocket of his jeans had looked like the surface of the moon.

She swung that spyglass around and looked through the big end. Her tiny husband looked a million miles away. What a great invention! So small, like an ant, a baby ant. That was Gavin, all right. He'd planned on being the only child forever. She straightened. He didn't deserve the sympathy he'd get if she burned his house down. Besides, what was the worst that could happen if she threw the pills away? Surely there was still one juicy little egg left inside her, protected on the bottom of the pile, and Mrs. McCall would never let him throw her out if she were pregnant.

She leaned her head on the window and knocked to get Gavin's attention. Ishmael had grabbed on to a coffin so as not to drown. She'd do better than that. Gavin turned round and round looking to see where the knocking was coming from, but didn't guess she'd be up so high.

§

Hillary O'Brian's
Cadillac Voices

Not everyone in Cadillac is pleased about having a town green. Here is a spirited criticism.

NOT SO FAST, MR. MAYOR

"Garden City," my aunt fanny! Mayor Mashburn's cockamamie scheme to tear down the old bowling alley and pool hall to build a town green, will kill what is left of business in downtown Cadillac. The mayor is telling everyone that the reason downtown is dead is because it has two boarded up properties right in the middle of it. Well, everyone knows that downtown is dead because of the Mall out on the highway with all that free parking.

I am one of the storeowners who already pays exorbitant rent to Mr. Murphy to keep my shop, Maxine's Ribbons and Bows, specializing in "those things that make a woman's heart glad." What we need is two city blocks of parking lot.

Mashburn says that if we have a town green, ice cream parlors and used bookstores will follow. I say if we have ice cream parlors and used bookstores we will have patrons dripping

ice cream on our goods and the kind of loiter-
ers you see on college campuses.

Maxine Graybill
Cadillac resident since 1963

THE SOLOIST
2011

So far Ryan and I, the minister, and of course Bryce, are the only ones present. Ryan has been worrying the minister about one more detail, but now he comes back toward the choir loft where I'm sitting. His new dark suit is so beautiful I want to reach down and touch it. He holds up a corsage—tiny white orchids.

"Ryan! What is this?"

"Please, Karen. Just put it on. And here." He hands me up a program. Bryce's picture is on the front. Inside are listed the order of the funeral service, including my two numbers, and the same remarks Ryan sent to the paper.

"What do you think?"

"Very nice," I say.

"They don't deserve all this."

"Where are they?" I ask.

"They've left the motel. That's all I know. I told his father, don't try to drive; you don't know Cadillac. Just take the cab. But old Buster probably never got in anything he wasn't driving himself, so I've been watching for a black Caddie." Ryan stares at Bryce's casket.

"How's his mother?"

Ryan shakes his head. "He wouldn't put her on the phone."

"Too upset?"

"He's never let me speak with her." He stops and glances up. "Please wear the corsage."

We both look back toward where the young black minister is gazing at the Hebrew symbols in one of the stained glass windows. This little church could have started out as a synagogue.

The whites of 's eyes look stark, Murine-bleached. He looks at the corsage. "I want everything to be perfect for them."

Why? I want to ask. Bryce made him promise he wouldn't send his body back to Abilene. So after everything else he's been through, Ryan had to fight Mr. Fry over that. And I hate to be a pain, but I ask, "Where's Belvedere? I can't sing "Wind Beneath My Wings" without an accompanist. There is no way."

Ryan's hands are up like a traffic cop, only they're shaking. "He's coming. He's coming. I double checked yesterday just before he left for the club."

"You don't know Belvedere. Mondays he sleeps all day."

Ryan has gotten thin this last year, though not as bad as Bryce. Ryan and I went to Cadillac High together. I pin on the corsage. "You look perfect, Karen," Ryan says. I knew he'd like the black dress and the hair up, my willowy lady look.

Ryan's the sort of guy who never stuck to anything

very long, but was good at whatever he tried. He worked in a men's shoe store until he got to be the top seller. Then he sold furniture, then drapery, and for a while he was a waiter in a swanky place. But he always moved on, leaving a trail of broken-hearted bosses behind. Until Bryce got sick.

I'm the real drifter, just floating along, letting my talents go to waste. I wait tables at the Ponderosa to pay the rent and sing at Starchy's when someone cancels, but I am nearly thirty, and though I've got a great voice, I haven't done one thing about it. Friends offer to help me make a demo, but I never take them up on it. The idea of putting something together kind of comes and goes. When I'm wearing my boots, dashing into the spotlight at Starchy's, with Bryce and Ryan standing, yelling, "Go, girl, go" — I can see it. But the very next night when I'm clearing a load of smeared up plates, dodging Buzz Halleck's greasy fingers, I can't see myself anywhere but the Ponderosa.

"I tried to get pallbearers," Ryan says. "I called. Some of our friends are — "

Jerks? I want to say. Wimps? Dead?

Ryan doesn't finish his sentence and wanders back toward the door. Three years he's had a florist shop out on the highway, working alone to save money for the meds.

Thank god, it's Belvedere, coming down the aisle, weaving just a little bit, dirty blond curls hanging in his pale blue eyes. But he's here. This is probably the first Monday morning he's seen in years. I just hope he's had something to drink. He opens the organ and begins to run the sleeve of his jacket back and forth along the keys to pick up the dust. He makes a quick selection of stops and looks down, situating his toes on the pedals.

A few more people have come in, a couple with a little boy. They must be neighbors. I don't recognize them. And six or eight black people. Ryan and Bryce used to give big parties in their fancy garden apartment. Bryce had money. Tons of people came to their parties, but there's not going to be any of them here today. Folks don't want to come down to this part of Cadillac. A place like this—down on Monroe Street—belongs to blacks and gays now. But Ryan loves it. They had real support in this chuch. He and Bryce came every Sunday till almost the end. "We're grown-ups now," Bryce said one night when they were in the Ponderosa. "We're learning to face reality together."

The minister is shaking hands with a big guy and a wife in a perfect black suit and a flash of diamonds. Ryan is fluttering; these must be the parents. Ryan escorts them to the front row where he has arranged little bouquets with ribbons to mark the first pews on either side. He sits down alone across the aisle.

Belvedere fires her up and after a little swerve, and a few adjustments of the stops, the old organ pours out a strong, steady progression of chords that remind me that this is a church. I fold back my program and place it on the music stand so Belvedere can see it. After the prayer I'm supposed to sing "This is My Father's World," a hymn I've been singing since I was three. I stand. This will help me warm up for the big production number Ryan wants at the end. Belvedere is going to be fine. The funeral is underway.

After I sit back down, I study Bryce's parents. She may be fifty, but she's still cute and innocent looking with that kind of soft blond hair we all wish we could afford. A rich man's sheltered doll. Ryan and Bryce have talked to me about Bryce's dad, but even if they hadn't, a guy who looks like old Buster wouldn't be any mystery to me. He went straight from being a big football hero at O.U. to tending his family's cattle and oil wells—one of those people who never stumbled, or if he did, he had Blondie there to cover for him. Mr. Fry has things his way. Once he found out Bryce was living with Ryan he cut off the money.

Ever since Mrs. Fry sat down she's been staring dry-eyed into the casket, her lips pressed into a little red line. Maybe only now is she giving up thoughts of grandchildren. The minister has spoken and we all sing "Abide With Me," but she keeps on staring. I wish the old guy would put his arm around her.

Belvedere is rolling out a grand prelude for my solo.

I bet the minister had no idea this organ could sound like the Mormon Tabernacle. I rise. My orchids flutter. My voice is full, a mezzo, and I don't see any reason just because this is a Disciples of Christ Church not to give it all I've got. I let it roll out, filling up the whole space, pressing on the stained glass windows, rising through the rafters. "Wind Beneath My Wings" is a number for the Broadway stage, but it always seemed to me to be a repentant song, to be sung to someone you're trying to make it up to. The kind of thing a woman wants to hear. As I near the last stanza, I open up, not louder, but more tender. I look at Mrs. Fry. Her face is breaking, wet and pink.

The minister gives a benediction and we rise. My first thought is to get out into the sunshine and warm up. Belvedere is playing "I Come to the Garden Alone," one of my old favorites. I take the program off the music stand and walk around to get out of the choir loft. As I step down, Mrs. Fry reaches out for me. I give her a hug, but she doesn't let go. "Oh, sweetheart," she sobs, and I let her fold against me. I rock her just a bit. Bryce was her only child. They say that nothing's harder in this whole world than losing a child. She is shorter than me, and she puts back her head to look up into my eyes. She takes a shuddery breath. "Bryce wrote and told me about you. He said he had fallen deeply in love. When I looked up there while you were singing and saw the tears in your eyes, I knew you were the one." She squeezes me good.

I look past her head at Buster Fry. His eyes are wide. His big rancher's hands are out. He's pleading. He's saying, just let this be. Just give her a brave smile and wave goodbye. He'd probably be willing to drive some kind of bargain for this sweet dream to come true. Mrs. Fry holds on. I used to fantasize about having rich, generous in-laws.

Ryan is standing across the aisle, his face white. He can't believe what he's hearing. But he shouldn't mind. This will comfort the poor bereaved mother, to think there's another grieving woman, someone who will miss her boy as much as she does. Ryan should want her to have this. He's never going to see these people again, anyway. What does he care? His hand reaches out to steady himself on the back of the pew. He will die too.

I watch him sit down, and I know that he's not going to fight this. The minister, standing in the back, hands clasped, waits for us to move on so he can let in the two men from the funeral home. In the absence of pallbearers, they will roll the casket up the aisle and load it into the hearse. I swallow hard.

I take Mrs. Fry gently by the shoulders and step back. "Mrs. Fry, I want you to meet Ryan Matthews. This is the person who supported Bryce when he had no money. Ryan carried him to see the doctor and fed him and cleaned him up. This is the man who asked me to come here today and sing. He wanted a nice funeral for you because you are Bryce's mother."

Ryan steps forward and holds out his hand. His lips are parted. Buster Fry's lower jaw has shoved forward. Mrs. Fry blinks to try to understand. I've blown away her lifelong shelter. She half turns toward Buster but catches his dark face and looks to me. I nod. She turns back and extends a trembling hand to Ryan. "I've waited a long time to meet you, Ryan."

I slip past them to go out into the sunshine. The minister follows and thanks me for my songs. "Do you sing professionally?" he asks.

I wrap my arms around myself. "No, not yet. But I will soon."

§

Hillary O'Brian's
Cadillac Voices

More thoughts about our Oklahoma weather and a surprising revelation about a favorite old song.

SAND

Lately there's been talk about Cadillac's climate in Hillary's column, and I'd like to speak up for myself and say I can take tornadoes and blizzards even the suffocating heat at midnight. But you want to know what just wears me out? The sand. It seeps in everywhere, around the windows, under the door and shakes off my little kids, their hair and shirts, gets caught in their pockets and between their toes. I'm not talking about dirt. It's that dad gum, powdery sand that blows in the air. "Here comes Texas," Mama used to say, squinting towards the west.

Woodie Guthrie was passing through Oklahoma during a sand storm, sky dark, everybody holding their noses like poison gas was coming. Thinking he was about to meet his Maker, Woodie wrote, "So Long, It's Been Good To Know You." I read that somewhere.

Big rollers like that don't come anymore

'cause of better farming and more lakes, but
when I see the sky around our place turn all
sour yellow and hear that singing the sand
makes as it scours the finish off our Dodge,
I think about my grandmother saying how
after a sand storm she'd sweep the dust off
the rafters before shaking out the curtains.
She'd wash each dish and every stitch of
clothes, and then round up her six kids for
Lifebuoy shampoos.

Estelle Barton
Ellis County resident since
1965

POWER BREAKFAST
2013

Wynona Blosser had always shown a terrible reverence for the power of money. Her excuse for why her son Floyd didn't graduate from high school, ever have a steady girl, or find any line of work, was that his daddy never gave him the reins over at the bank. So now that Old Blosser was dead, she was just standing back waiting for her little Floyd to blossom into a shrewd businessman and civic leader.

Floyd himself hadn't changed a bit since his daddy died. Thirty-six years old and the heir to millions, big old, soft Floyd still shambled around in the fancy clothes his mother picked out and acted embarrassed not to have jeans and a greasy windbreaker like the rest of us.

It was everybody else here at the coffee shop who'd changed. Used to be Murleen brought Floyd the mop when he spilled milk, and here she was this morning, straining the seams of an unusually clean waitress uniform, asking if she couldn't get him a little more butter for his flapjacks.

And Peanuts Murphy, that balding curmudgeon, still fuming about the way the town fathers had tried to cheat him last week, said he was going to show everyone in town with a much bigger project. He was proposing himself and Floyd be partners in a development scheme to dam up the Fuller creek and build a high-end lakeside addition. This partnership was to be 50-50, of course: Floyd would put up all the money, Peanuts would do all the thinking.

I was disgusted. Everybody in Cadillac seemed to be holding their breath, waiting for Floyd to write that first misguided check and prove us all right about him. We figured this was the beginning of the end of the Blosser fortune, and while it was getting frittered away, we might as well stand up close, so some of it frittered onto us.

I am a good case in point. Truth to tell, the very first thing I thought of when I heard about old Blosser bending forward in agony in the barber's chair, was the busted clutch plate on my pickup—$400.00 right there. Floyd missed my truck. So did I, of course. I hate bumming rides, and Floyd missed riding out to the creek to fish and shoot jackrabbits.

The problem was getting a word in edgewise. Peanuts, sweat glistening on his bald head, was bulling on about subcontractors and earth moving. Murleen wanted a life-long meal ticket, and the preacher, damn his greedy hide, had already proposed that Floyd might want to put aluminum siding on the parsonage—just as a memorial to old Blosser. Jesus!

Peanuts was talking "recreational use" when Floyd

stood up from the table like he'd had a sudden call from nature. "R.J.," he called over to me, "could I see you outside? Please?"

"Hold on now, Floyd," Peanuts said, "we've got business to transact."

"I know," said Floyd, "but I've got to go right now." And he got up with the paper napkin still stuck in the front of his shirt. I pulled the napkin out, dropped it on a table and pushed open the door for Floyd.

"R.J., can we go out to the creek?" Floyd asked when we got outside.

"Sorry, Floyd, the clutch is shot."

"Let's take a car then."

"Axles're too low. You know that."

"I need to talk to you. I'm worried about the money."

"Yeah. I know. Just keep it all. Don't sign anything, especially with Peanuts."

"I wasn't going to. Peanuts is okay, but I like the creek."

"Atta boy. Reach out and take what you want."

"The problem is, I think I already signed something. I think the money's all gone."

"My god, Floyd, what happened?"

"Can't we go out to the creek? How long will it take Buddy to put in a new clutch?"

"I don't know. He ain't even towed it yet."

"Call him up. Tell him to go get it. Tell him I'll pay."

"But you just said all your money was gone."

"Buddy doesn't know that yet."

I was amazed. Maybe Mrs. Blosser was right. Maybe her little boy was smartening up.

It was hard to believe that a stranger had gotten to Floyd before any of us hometown boys, but as he stammered out the story two days later while we sat on a log beside the creek, it became clear that's exactly what had happened. Floyd stared at his shiny loafers and told how the day after the funeral, passing himself off as a financial planner, a man from Tulsa had persuaded Floyd to sign over 3.6 million dollars to be invested in some kind of securities. Floyd's account at the bank registered empty, and he was too ashamed to tell anyone.

I asked if he had a copy of what he'd signed, and he pulled a little wad of paper out of the side pocket of his sport coat. He'd folded the thing about a dozen times, the way a grade school kid does, so I had a hard time opening it up without tearing it. I read it but couldn't tell much. Floyd's blocky signature was in three different places, and this guy, Giacometti, had also signed it, but these things aren't my line.

"Is this all the money there was?" I asked.

"Daddy had been selling things, houses and his interest in the paint store and the barber shop to get cash for some deal, Mama said. So when he died, it was all there in the bank."

"Oh, brother."

"Everybody's going to laugh," he whimpered.

"Maybe this guy's on the level. Maybe he's out there making money for you right now."

Floyd just shook his head. More than anybody else in town, he'd known he'd lose it. He wiped his nose with a clean white handkerchief. "I just didn't think it'd be this fast," he said. "I was going to give you a real good fishing rod and buy Peanuts a DVD. Murleen wants a diamond ring."

"There's one good thing—you're not going to get tangled up with Murleen. Just tell folks your investments didn't pan out and then shut up."

"No, you tell them. I've got to tell Mama."

"At least this will get Peanuts off your back."

We left it at that. I only told one person, and I picked him very carefully. I waited until I ran into him coming out of the hardware store the next afternoon.

"Hello, Reverend Fletcher, how're you."

"Very well, thank you, which is always a blessing at my age."

"I haven't seen you since Blosser's funeral," I said.

"My, my what a tragedy—so young, only 81, and such a generous man. He will be missed."

"Yeah, it's a shame about his money."

"What do you mean, R.J.?" The reverend pulled his chin down and looked at me through his eyebrows.

"Floyd said it was just one bad investment."

Fletcher's nostrils flared, and he got a little green around the gills. "You mean Floyd's lost all the money already."

"Yep. Easy come, easy go, huh, Reverend?" I did feel a little mean, but I wanted to see the look on his face as he saw that aluminum siding go a-glimmering. What a dark thing my heart is.

That was around five p.m. At 7:30 the next morning we were gathered at the front corner table of The Busy Bee, and Floyd asked Murleen for some catsup for his eggs. She told him to get it himself.

And that would have been it, end of story. But three weeks later I got a very shaky-voiced call from Floyd who told me he'd just gotten some little pieces of paper from New York, and it looked like all his money was resting comfortably there in a brokerage house in his name.

I told Floyd to keep the news to himself, but he couldn't bear not to have everybody slobber over him.

The wolves closed in. Murleen shined up her act with a new hair-do and some clothes that would have made a saloon girl proud. Peanuts got my boss, Karl Stolt, to draw up plans and estimates for the dam on assurances that Floyd would, when the time came, sign anything Peanuts told him to. Reverend Fletcher put Floyd on the church Building Committee. And Mother Blosser brought in her contender for the wife of the heir, the grandchild of a friend of hers. She moved Gretchen into their house and made it clear that nature could take its course. Floyd was bewildered. We spent a lot of time at the creek.

"Reach out and take hold," I said. "Decide what you really want, and go for it."

Talk is cheap. I felt sorry for him, but I also couldn't resist making things a little worse. The idea came to me in a flash, and I leaned over to Floyd who was sitting there on the log, with his arms around his knees like an oversized six-year-old on a slop jar. "Floyd," I whispered, "if you're really going to haul off and refuse to sign the contract for the dam like you're saying, then I think you ought to invite your Mother and little Gretchen to join you for breakfast at The Busy Bee. Just for moral support."

"Really," he said, amazed.

"Really."

"You come too, okay?"

I wasn't the only one with a flare for drama. When the morning of the showdown came, Peanuts brought a kid with a camera and my friend Hillary from *The Courier*. He also brought my boss, Karl Stolt, a ham-fisted guy who always had breakfast at home. I didn't offer any pleasantries. We all sat down at the long table in the front window and waited. I hoped this would be quick since I was hungry.

When Gretchen walked in, towed by Wynona Blosser, I knew I was in the presence of the kind of slim, washed-out young female you almost never see anymore. Gretchen stared around The Busy Bee with parted lips and vacant eyes, a real empty cup, one of that vanishing breed who respects anything that's bigger or older than she is just so long as it's male. The perfect woman for Floyd.

Mrs. Blosser, ruddy with rouge and clanking with gold jewelry, guided Gretchen, almost transparent by comparison, to the seat next to Floyd. I was sitting on the other side of Floyd, our backs to the window. Karl Stolt, Peanuts, and a lawyer named Wallingford faced us. Except for taking a light reading off Peanuts' forehead, the photographer and the reporter waited motionless in the corner.

Murleen wore a tight, white dress that came half way down her thighs. And slung kitty-cornered across her lumpy hips was a turquoise Indian belt, heavy enough to carry six-shooters. She seemed anxious about what her role might be, and armed with the coffee pot, she hovered. Our sheriff, Jake Hale, who liked to eat in peace, took one look at the big set up and left.

The first one to make a move was Wynona Blosser. She stood up and shook hands with Peanuts, Stolt, and Wallingford and paid each one some flimsy compliment about knowing his sisters or admiring his rose bushes.

It was at that point that it first crossed my mind that she might not be entirely against flooding forty fertile acres in order to have lake front property for expensive houses.

She sat back, real proud to have gotten us clods off to a gracious start. I wanted Peanuts to say, Sign here, so that Floyd could say no, like he wanted, and we could all order breakfast. But Wallingford began to drone on in that legal talk that puts everyone to sleep. You just have to let those guys run down, so I waited and kept checking Floyd's face. He had that same shut-down look he used to get from algebra. But Wynona kept piping up with uh huhs and absolutelies. She really liked this stuff, and she may have even understood it. I couldn't say. My stomach growled.

I realized then that this deal might be a dumb idea for seventeen different reasons, but if the Widow Blosser found it entertaining and socially to her advantage, well we might as well sell those guns we'd been shooting jack rabbits with and buy ourselves some boats.

Finally Wallingford was winding down. Peanuts snapped the button on his ballpoint and placed his fingers on the edge of his papers, ready to push them across the table to Floyd. Stolt kept rocking his elbows on the table. He'd had a belly full of party-of-the-first-parts, and he'd looked at the Coca Cola clock about thirty times. I knew he was counting every minute that he wasn't riding herd on his crew.

Suddenly Mrs. Blosser took over again. "I know none of us wants this to be just an ordinary development. The quality of the detail in these houses must be the very finest. Kitchen cabinets, for instance. And this town could use a new country club, which would make a wonderful center of the development."

This was too much for Stolt. He slammed down his fist. "Are you gonna sign this or not!" he shouted at Floyd. Murleen, always sensitive to the direction of the wind, was standing behind Stolt. "Sign it!" she said with a swagger of the holster belt.

Floyd looked at his mother, who gave him back a forty-caliber smile that caused his head to sink a little further into his chest. Peanuts shoved the papers across and put the pen in Floyd's left hand. I waited for Floyd to turn my way. I would at least have given him the raising of my eyebrows: Is this really what you want? But his gaze wouldn't rise off the table. He was ashamed. I heard him inhale. He straightened the papers and looked for the big X's to which Peanuts was directing his attention.

But before he put the pen to the paper, Floyd stopped, statue still. I don't think the man was breathing. Then there was a tremor in his body, like a very mild earthquake that shakes every particle just a little. His head was rising up from his chest. I looked across his lap to see his right hand resting on Gretchen's narrow thigh. Not just resting, actually. He had a good grip on

108

her around the inside near the knee. I leaned forward to see her face. She was looking straight ahead, wide eyes on the high beam.

"Peanuts," Floyd said slow and tight, "you are my friend, but I don't want to dam up the creek." With that he screeched back from the table. I thought he might haul Gretchen out by the thigh, but he released her, and the two of them rushed out, leaving Mother Blosser to cover their backs. And I have got to hand it to her, the lady did a real fine job.

Peanuts reared back into Murleen and the coffee pot. "Sonovabitch! Floyd, you get back in here!" The coffee went mostly on Wallingford, who was trying to save himself and his paperwork. The photographer was snapping wildly and Hillary was grinning. Peanuts headed for the door, but Wynona blocked it. She may have been entertained by legal talk, but the sight of her cub standing up to the lawyer, the contractor and the developer put fire in the lioness's eyes.

"Sit down!" she roared at Peanuts. "Floyd has spoken."

Wow! Floyd and Gretchen were off, probably looking for a spot where he could get another good grip on her. Stolt headed out through the kitchen. Wallingford still sat at the table, mopping off the contracts with a handful of paper napkins, and Murleen, with coffee on her tits, posed for pictures.

Mrs. Blosser had backed Peanuts into a chair. The

poor man was livid. Twice in ten days his big plans had fallen through. There would be no living with him now. I figured it was not a good day to show up to work for Karl Stolt, so I just sat back and ordered some eggs and hash browns, those being, at the time, what I wanted to reach out and grab hold of.

§

Hillary O'Brian's
Cadillac Voices

The arts are alive and boiling in Cadillac.

POET LAUREATE

Who told you people you needed a poet laureate? And who told you this was the way to find one—run a contest and let the president of the garden club choose the winner?

They've asked me to compete with a couple of jingle writers, a Hallmark alum and the composer of Hop-a-long hymns. This is not proper competition for a man who has published his work in *Poets Carnival*.

I am ashamed to admit how pleased I was when the dean of fine arts at CC College asked me if he could advance my name for Poet Laureate. I fell all over myself, not even asking Laureate of what. We poets can get excited over crumbs—like my sonnet in *The Courier* printed next to a recipe for Apple Pan Dowdy.

Now this. Do I send a villanelle just to make sure I will be misunderstood and can retire with hauteur when I lose? Or shall I grovel—write some rhyming suck-up in praise of the prairie?

I am tortured.

My wife tells me I would be tortured if I lived in Boston and published in *The Paris Review.*

It's true. But humiliation is my muse. This insult is like kindling. I will catch, flare, and warm the cheeks of Madame President of the Garden Club. One takes one's audience where one finds her.

Herbert Ashcroft Wiley
Cadillac resident since 1990

Farley's is a huge hardware store, open seven days a week 'til ten. They sell lumber, barbecues, unpainted furniture, shower curtains and telephones. Farley's is my secret ace in the hole; I call it "Hillary's Refuge." When I become too shaky about being alone, I come down to Farley's where "Everything to Make an Oklahoma House a Home" is on sale. Besides that, all the products come with instructions. And failing those, they offer a courteous staff of men who will explain everything.

But this afternoon is not one of those shaky times. I have a couple of hours before Jenny gets home from school, and I'm going to check on a picnic table with benches attached—a clearance item. I seem to be the only customer interested in this bargain—$69.95, redwood. A bony-faced clerk with slicked-back black hair is standing beside the floor sample. His name, Morgan, is stitched on his white Farley's shirt. I hope he will move on, but he just folds his broad arms across his chest. The picnic set is a satisfying, dark rose color, sanded smooth. "What I'm looking for," I say, "is a kind of booth effect. For my kitchen?"

The manager frowns.

"A cozy corner to eat in, sort of enclosed, you know,

with a lamp overhead, in front of a window, a good place for homework too."

Morgan's frown deepens.

"I don't have any kitchen furniture," I say. "This would be a start, wouldn't it? For the time being."

He is shaking his head. "I wouldn't," he says.

"You wouldn't, huh? Well, what would you do?" I sound strident. Morgan glances down the aisle to see if anyone has heard the unhappy customer.

"You'd have to build in something like that," he says softly. He keeps his arms folded, and tightens his grip on the muscles beneath his rolled up sleeves. Damn him. If I were handy, I wouldn't be considering such a stopgap solution.

"Your husband could —"

"My husband was a salesman. Salesmen don't build things. Robert never fixed a thing in his life. Salesmen play golf!" I am trembling. I turn and make myself walk briskly towards the exit.

I sit in my car in the parking lot and wait for the hot spinning behind my breast bone to slow. I am weakened against these outbursts partly because I seem to have lost the knack of sleeping at night. At first after Robert left, I thought the problem was in our bed. I took Jenny and stayed a few nights with my folks.

"Did you sleep?" my father would ask each morning.

"No."

114

"But you rested, right?" As though my time in bed were idle. We went back to our house, where I could not sleep in private. I tried all the tricks — exercised myself to exhaustion, drank warm milk, thought happy thoughts as I set aside my book and switched off the lamp. Then, suddenly the dark would harness me to a wheel — *If I'd known the rules had changed, Robert, I would have played a different game! — a better game — If I'd known you'd changed the rules on me, Robert. You changed, Robert —* round and round I tread the same circle. *If I'd known that was how we were going to conduct ourselves. Robert!*

It is hot in the car. I turn on the engine, set the air-conditioning on high, and try to get a grip. I am Hillary O'Brian, a long time resident of Cadillac. I am now a journalist with a new job, hot on my first important story. I am a homeowner. I vote, pay my bills, and most of all, I am a mother, and I must not let myself fall apart in public.

The school bus lets Jenny off just before the road dips between us and the section line. Although she's still half a mile away, I can watch her coming home from her first day of school. She's only ten, a new fifth grader, but there are already signs that she's going to be built just like me — not a sprinter, a bit of a trudger, but she's picking up a little speed. I dry my hands and head for the back door.

"Guess what," she says as she plunks her papers on the card table next to my typewriter and reaches for the fridge. "Mr. Richter, my teacher, he isn't married."

"Yes, I know." I actually was at O.U. at the same time Todd Richter was regarded as the cutest football player in A House.

"Mom!" She turns from the fridge with a can of coke in hand. Her eyes are wide with excitement. "He's extremely handsome, and he's just your age!"

We stand there facing each other. She thinks I'm slow to get her point. I suddenly feel very heavy — "good farming stock," I once heard my father say referring to that side of the family I have to thank for most of my physical characteristics. Jenny's eyes are bright with her news. She is ready to conspire. She thinks we will sit down now to decide what outfit I will wear on my date with Mr. Richter. Jenny is too young, I think, to be introduced to the concept of a woman's market value.

"Sit down, hon. Catch your breath. Do you have any homework?" I sit on my mother's old dresser bench that I use while typing at the card table.

Jenny sits on the piano stool across from me. "Don't you want to talk about Mr. Richter?"

"Surely there're lots of other things to talk about. What'd they give you for lunch?"

She is suddenly glum. "Meat loaf," she says hardly moving her lips. I've handled this wrong. All summer

116

she's been on the lookout for a good man, and today she found the perfect answer for revenge. Her daddy married a new wife and moved three hundred miles away. She hates him. She misses him desperately. This would have shown him. We found somebody better—a handsome teacher, a man who can play the guitar, a man who wears jeans and boots to school. But stupid Mom has smashed it. Jenny twists off the piano stool, anxious to go upstairs and get on the phone to a friend. I've been so eager for her to come home, and she hasn't been in the kitchen five minutes.

"I'm going to make tacos for supper," I call after her. I pull my laptop in front of me. I need to finish the piece on the City Commission's input on the town green proposition before I start supper. Mr. Tarman has me on probation to see if I can handle a story with a death and a Las Vegas widow. But this is my story, and I can barely wait to pounce on the toxic waste issue.

In the morning I rise from the labors of the night and prepare for my day job. I drop Jenny at school, then head for my desk at work. This job is getting exciting, poking underneath Cadillac's self-satisfied, booster surface.

I stop in at Farley's on the way home for light bulbs. I must not start avoiding this place. I dash down the center aisle and make a left. There seems to be nothing here but paint, stacked to the ceiling—canyon-like, running for miles in either direction. Dammit, where are the light bulbs. I whip around a corner and bump into Morgan.

"Gosh, I'm sorry," he says.

"I'm sorry. Really." We have jumped back from each other.

"Pews may be the answer," he says.

"What?"

"You asked what I would do for the kitchen?"

"Thank you, Morgan." I am still catching my breath. Maybe this is one of those very literal-minded people who thinks you really want to know when you ask, How are you? Light bulbs. Light bulbs. Just don't get into another scene. I make myself smile. "Thanks, really."

"No," he says holding up his hands.

"Pews?" I ask.

"My old church is auctioning off the pews to raise money for the building fund. You could just look at them, maybe get some ideas."

"Where?"

"Up near Bartlesville. Saturday morning."

"That's a long way."

"I could show you. I'm going anyway." He hands me his card. Morgan Thornton, General Manager.

Friday afternoon Jenny comes in, but doesn't speak. She has taken forever to get up the hill, and I know there is bad news. She gets a soda from the refrigerator, but doesn't sit down. Her face is pinched shut.

"So how was school?"

With great concentration, she opens the pull tab. "Mr. Richter is taking Patty Morrison's mom to Oklahoma City to a Miranda Lambert concert."

Well of course he is, I want to say. She's just his type, poor thing. Jenny looks up. She's crying. The good man has gotten away. "Ah, sweetie, don't cry." I rush toward her. She pulls away and runs upstairs. I lean on the card table and let myself down in front of the laptop. I rest my fingers on the keyboard.

Todd Richter was a second string football player, but he was handsome enough to glide along in that social strata where warm, sweet breaths encouraged him to believe that his luck would somehow carry him right into the pros. But when O.U. gets done with its jocks, they often discover that they are not young gods, but grade school teachers— elementary education being an easy major.

By 11:00 p.m. I am drowsy. I must let sleep slip over me like a net over a dumb animal. I stretch and close my eyes. *"You must have had a good laugh, Robert— me humming along, no clue. What a laugh, Robert!"*

Cars are parked on both sides of the country road for half a mile. How did all these people find out about an auction at a country church? As we pull up, a man says hello to Morgan and takes aside a rope that has kept people from parking in the churchyard. It's a pretty church, bigger than I'd expected. The auctioneer has set up a platform with a podium. There are folding chairs, but many people are sitting on the pews, drinking from Styrofoam cups and eating donuts.

Morgan parks behind the church. I can tell already, this isn't going to work. These pews are too big for my kitchen—dark, clumsy things, gummy with age. They look out of place, like beached whales out of their dim, cool element; slung out in the bright sun where people gawk at their scars. "Come on," Morgan says. These are his first words in an hour.

It had been dark when his new pickup pulled in front of my house. We dropped Jenny at Patty's and drove over three hours. He has what my dad calls a hatchet face— narrow with high cheek bones and a hook nose, proba- bly some Indian blood. He told me this was his boyhood church, but he moved to Cadillac after he finished busi- ness school at O.U. Not much information for a over two hundred miles. I didn't ask him if he knew Robert in the business school or if he'd heard of Todd Richter.

"Do you want to look inside first?" he asks. We climb the three steps of the old clapboard church and stand in the doorway. There is the smell of old hymnals and recent carpentry. The morning sunlight streams through the dusty air into the bare, empty space. On the floor dark holes mark where each pew was unbolted. The chancel, without its pulpit or choir, looks to be nothing but a stage, its holiness stripped away. Only the walls are left—a carcass without its bones. There is a story here. "Can't you use the pews in the new church?"

"The majority voted for theater seats." He says this evenly, looking straight ahead. "Theater seats and air conditioning is what this is all about." His jaw pulses leaving me sure how he would have voted if he'd still lived here. "When I was first divorced," he says, "I felt just like this church—a big old drafty hollow thing that had lost its purpose."

He escorts me out to a pew in the shade of a big elm tree then heads in the direction of the auctioneer. I hadn't thought about whether he'd ever been married.

I had known Todd Richter at O.U. and actually spoke to him once. It was one of those brief interludes that occurs at the end of the semester between the good-looking guy who's hardly attended class and the female grind he approaches for her botany notes.

I feel myself smiling now and straighten in the pew to lift my elbow to see that on the armrest there is a band of carving—a twisting pattern. Fish—gracefully swimming down the armrest. They have long curved bodies like salmon, their backs smoothed by generations of churchgoers whose fingers have traced their silky progress through thousands of sermons. I want this pew. It is comforting. Its gentle curves are better than any fine furniture. It will bring dignity and stability to my home. I look up. Morgan is coming back. He's got to tell me how to get this.

"You may not like these particular pews," Morgan says and hands me a cup of coffee and a donut. "There are some from the choir—shorter."

I want to look for them, but the bidding has already started. "Forty, Gemme fifty. Forty, Gemme fifty. Got fifty. Who'll Gemme sixty," the auctioneer chants.

"It's buy the piece and take the pair," Morgan says softly.

"What does that mean?"

"They are selling them in twos. The price reached in the bidding is for one."

"So whatever I bid, I will pay twice that, right?"

"Right."

I will wait for the choir pews.

I had been in one of my reckless frames of mind when I picked up the phone and called him. It was one of those what-the-hell-nothing-else-is-happening-in-my-social-life moments. The association with Farley's probably gave him a warranty of safety: This is not a strangler. He told me to bring cash just in case I wanted to bid. I have three hundred dollars in my purse. Numbers seventy-nine and eighty have just sold for a hundred and ten dollars apiece. Morgan is leaning forward, his elbows on his knees. His thin lips are pressed shut, his hatchet profile is harsh. "We've got to do better than this," he says. Of course, this was his church. He wants the bids to go higher. It is only 9:30.

By noon all the long pews have been sold. I feel grateful that after a steady rise, the price has come down, but Morgan is leaning forward, his big hands gripped. He rises when an old couple comes up to thank him for his help. I stand aside and listen. Morgan was in charge of removing the pews. He stoops slightly to listen to the couple. Jenny had spurned his gentle greeting this morning, making it clear that the only exciting possibilities for the day awaited at Patty's.

After lunch one of the smaller choir pews is lifted onto the platform beside the auctioneer. Number three. It looks rosy in the sunlight, not like the long ones. I turn to look at Morgan. "I rubbed it down with Murphy's soap and steel wool," he says. The crowd is scurrying to their seats. "Buy the piece and take the pair," shouts the auctioneer to start things off. "Who'll gemme a hunnert, Gemme a hunnert, Gemme a hunnert," begins his nasal chant. "Gotta hunnert. Who'll Gemme hunnert twenty. Got twenty. Got thirty. Got forty. Got fifty."

Oh, no. I'm out of it, and I didn't even get to bid.

Morgan is sitting up very tall turning his head from bidder to bidder. He is smiling. The final bid is seven hundred.

On the long drive home I keep wanting to say, Listen, Mr. Handyman, why didn't you suggest I buy two of the long ones and cut them down? Why did you let me wait for those choir pews?

It's only five when we get back to Cadillac. "I want to show you something," he says as we pull onto Ellis Street. "Can we stop a minute at my place?"

I'm hot and tired and eager to get Jenny and try to forget about redoing my kitchen. "Gee, can it wait?" I say. "I really have to pick up Jenny and get home."

Two nights later Morgan calls. He is taking a break at work, and I can tell from his tone that he wants to shoot the breeze awhile. Jenny and I are in the middle of dinner, and she stares at me as I try to make casual conversation standing at the wall phone beside the sink. I feel like I am trying to talk to a boy with my mother listening, but Morgan's deep voice contains no push or program, and it comforts me.

"Not that hardware guy?" Jenny asks when I hang up. The expression on her face makes me want to slap her, but I don't. Mothers are supposed to be constant, placid, sexless beings. Tomorrow I will choose another Voice for my column and hand it to Mr. Tarman.

Farley's seven-days-a-week, fifteen-hour-days leave Morgan almost no free time, but we talk on the phone every day. He's good at asking questions and then waiting while I meander and double back into my answers. I like his sense of humor. He's a farm boy—doesn't shy away from alluding to cow pies and prairie oysters. Yet he can be subtle. Tonight I asked him if he liked fishing.

"Fishing, huh?" he draws out the words. "Yeah, I can fish."

"Oh," I say, "and what kind of a fisherman are you?"

"I'm a fly fisher."

"Oh?"

"Fly fishermen are very particular. I'm not a trawler." His voice is deep and slow, and I cannot get enough of it. He says, "Never had any taste for just dragging the net along behind the boat. I won't sample something just because it jumps into my net, looking flashy."

I close my eyes and press my forehead against the kitchen wall to savor a moist pang rising in me that I had forgotten I could feel. "We fly fishermen know what we want," he says. "And we tie a fly, something subtle, irresistible, tailor-made to get the job done. And we have to go to just the right pool where the particular fish we want swims. And we stand there in the cold water, patiently sending out our line as long as it takes to entice the one we have set our hearts on." There is silence now on the line, and I know he can hear me breathing.

It's Sunday morning. The phone is ringing. Jenny is spending the night at Patty's house. She and I packed a dress and the patent leather flats for Sunday school. This is all coming back as I struggle to rise from a deep pool of sleep. I feel almost too heavy to swim or to raise my head to look at the clock. 7:20. I pick up the phone. Jenny says I must come get her immediately. What has gone wrong? I throw on my jeans and rush into town without even brushing my teeth.

In the car she sits as far from me as she can get. I know she will run to her room as soon as we get inside, so I step in the back door ahead of her and block her path to the stairs. She sits on the piano stool and wraps her arms around her waist. Finally she looks at me. "Mom, I made a bad mistake."

"What happened, sweetheart?" My heart is thumping.

She turns slightly and looks at the floor. "Mr. Richter—you know how I wanted you to go out with him?"

"Yes, sweetheart, I know."

She glances sidelong at me and her chin quivers. I kneel beside her. "I thought he was so wonderful, and—" She gulps and lets me take her in my arms. "I thought he was a nice person, but he did something that hurt Patty's mom's feelings, and now she's crying all night. He's so nice in school—" She drags in a shaky breath and then in a hot sob, "I hate him."

"Oh, sweetheart." Oh god, here it is. I struggle not to cry with her.

"Listen, Jenny." I hold her back from me and look

her in the eye. "I'm the one who made the mistake. When you wanted me to go out with Mr. Richter, I knew he wouldn't ask me out, and that made me feel so bad for you that I forgot to tell you that I didn't even want to go out with him."

She looks at me, incredulous, still shaking. "Why not?"

"Well, I'll tell you, honey, my guess is that Mr. Richter has always been a popular guy—in college and high school and maybe even when he was your age." I stop and swallow. She's waiting. "Well, sometimes when a person is that popular and good-looking and has people falling all over them from the beginning, he just never learns how to deserve friends—how to be a really good friend. And, sometimes, he just winds up hurting people, like Patty's mom."

"You're saying he's a jerk?" Her gaze is direct through her watery eyes.

"Yes. That's what I'm saying."

Her face twists, but she presses her lips together and gives a couple of quick nods. She will try to see this.

Morgan picks us up in his truck on a Saturday morning. I told Jenny that I wanted to go see his house, and that he had a cat she could play with if she wanted to come along. She's been very quiet all week. She and I have agreed that she is doing very well in school, that she has a good teacher. She struggles to reconcile love and hate for Todd Richter and for her father. I wish she were a baby again, so I could rock her to soothe the pain.

Morgan's house, a small ranch like the others on its street, has two spindly oaks in front, each circled by a heavy wreath of fine mulch. A garden hose is coiled on a shiny, wheeled rack beside the driveway. The place looks like a Farley's ad in the Sunday magazine section.

A gray and white cat is waiting on the porch and, like a good hostess, she trots up to meet Jenny. "Come around in the back," Morgan says to the two of them. On the cement back steps a bag of kibble has been placed. Morgan stoops down, takes a bit of kibble between his thumb and middle finger and holds it above the cat's nose. The cat sits back on her hind legs and raises her front paws with the pads together as though she is praying. "That's right," he says, "say the blessing." Then he tosses the kibble in the air, and like a show dog the cat leaps and seizes it.

"My goodness," I say, "that's evidence of a very smart cat."

He hands the bag of kibble to Jenny, and he and I start in the back door. "That's evidence," he says quietly to me, "of a man with too much time on his hands."

Inside the house looks bare, unlived-in. The flecked beige kitchen wallpaper looks like something chosen by a computer. He ushers me down the basement steps and flips on a large, overhead fluorescent light. As the bulbs flicker and light up, I see that before us, sitting on a heavy white drop cloth, is a beautiful little cherry choir pew. I gasp. The old finish has been rubbed to a soft, rosy glow. In the corner is another, its surface still dark, its base broken so badly that one end of the seat rests on the floor.

"Numbers one and two," I say softly. I had meant to ask where they were.

"They got wrecked in the removal. The fools just started rocking them. That's when they called me. The auctioneer wouldn't take these, so I gave the church a hundred dollars for each and put all the pieces in the truck. This one is almost finished." He runs his long fingers down the curved arm. I see now that there are still pipe clamps attached to the bases.

"Can the other one be restored?"

"Oh sure, it's not so bad off as this one was. Only one end is splintered. I'll have them finished up by next week if you're interested."

"Yes, yes!" I press fingers against the carving—bread and wine.

"The other one's got the fish," he says.

"Why didn't you just bring me here first, before the auction?"

"I wasn't sure I was going to let you have them." He smiles. "And I wanted to get to know you better, mostly have you get to know me. I knew Robert in school, but didn't know you were divorced until that day in the store—when you got going about salesmen playing golf." He grins.

"So, at the auction, what did you think?"

"Well," he says slowly, "Hillary, even if I hadn't liked what I found—" He stops, glances at the floor, then looks up, "you were such a feast to look at."

I'm stunned. It is the first extravagant thing he's said. My cheeks burn.

"What's going on?" It is Jenny standing at the top of the stairs. The cat appears, curving around the leg of her jeans.

"Hi, hon, come on down," I say.

She looks soberly from one of us to the other and begins to step slowly down the stairs.

"Jenny," Morgan says, "your mother and I are about to strike a bargain." He says this gravely. Jenny's eyes widen. She steps heavily off the last step and comes to stand beside me. The cat follows, and she picks her up. "I'm making her an offer," he says.

I fumble to open my purse. "Three hundred," I say.

"Two hundred," he says.

"Three hundred," I say, opening my checkbook, "delivered and installed." He frowns. "Take it or leave it," I say. Jenny frowns at us as she struggles to hold the weight of the large, purring cat.

"I don't know, lady," Morgan draws his chin down and gives me a business-like look, "whether you're aware of what you're getting into. This kind of furniture," he says turning now to Jenny, "can't be rearranged all the time, you know."

I watch his face. "These pews—" he says looking dead level back at me, "we'll have to bolt them down— right through your floor joists."

"Oh?" I say, giving him the arch of my eyebrow.

"Represents a major commitment." He's still trying to deadpan it, but his nostrils flare with the effort.

"That's all right," Jenny says, "we trust you." She shifts the load of the cat up onto her shoulder and starts back up the stairs. She seems to have decided it's all right to leave us alone.

§

Hillary O'Brian's
Cadillac Voices

Here's a piece about a smart man in the right place at the right time, who knew how to take advantage of what fortune brought him. Sounds like the Donald Trump of his day.

A MAN OF VISION

So many of the folks are new here in Cadillac, so they probably don't know about the kind of men that built up this great state—men like my granddaddy, J.J. McAlester. They don't make 'em like granddaddy anymore. Vision! Let me tell you.

He came to Oklahoma a young man, and first thing found himself a pretty little Arapaho maiden to marry. The Arapahos had their own nation, see? And were, of course, thrilled to have a fine young white man like Granddaddy become a citizen of their nation. And being a citizen, Granddaddy had the advantage of one of their laws that said a man could own as much land as he could fence. See? He got all his new Indian "brothers" to help him fence in two thousand acres of tribal lands, and here's the vision part, it was land around the route he'd heard the railroad was going to take.

Now my granddaddy wasn't one to be idle, so while he waited for the tracks to make their way in his direction, he hosted hunting parties for gentry in the woods on his property. While guiding a bunch of wealthy Minnesotans on a wild turkey shoot, Granddaddy discovered what looked like coal land. Everyone kept mum while they waited for a geologist and lined up investors back East.

And while he's waiting on all that, Granddaddy built a dry goods store, a grocery, a livery stable, a hotel, a funeral parlor, and, for the convenience of his customers, a wagon lot. And seeing what a good job he was doing of building up the town, the Federal government set up one of its Tribal Lands Offices there and the State made it the home of its largest prison. Payroll was insured. So when the railroad did come through, Old J.J. was sitting pretty. And after statehood in 1907, they named the town after him.

And you ask, what about the coal? Well, shoot, those mines, to this very day are producing much of Oklahoma's electricity and will be way into the 21st Century. Vision!

Luther McAlester
Cadillac resident since 1960

Last Saturday night, the 27th, the four of us went to the movie as usual. Afterwards, no more than an hour after we dropped off Toots and Ray at home, our phone rang and Toots said, "Get over here!" Her voice sounded like the strangled whisper of a woman hiding in a closet. I said, "Where's Ray?" "He's here," she answered.

I was speechless.

First and foremost, you know that Ray Ketcham is my best friend. He and his wife, Toots, and me and my Carol have been pals the better part of this century. So Carol and I rushed over to their place expecting something horrible, but by the time we got there, Ray was just sitting there beneath this big dent in his wall checking the scores on their big old tube television. He said it was all a false alarm, and Toots had gone to bed. We've known Toots all her life, so we could almost believe she was nutty enough to have made a frantic call for help, then decided to go to bed before we could get there.

You know what a funny thing Toots is—all that energy jumping around in her skinny little body. When she was a girl, she put me in mind of a Fourth of July sparkler, shooting out in all directions, lighting up any group she was in. Weightless and flighty, she looked inexhaustible to us boys who were crazy with hope she'd drop a few sparks on us. Now she's older, the sparkle is gone, but she's still energetic, fidgety really. And her voice, of course, has tightened up a turn or two, so the ripple is gone.

Carol and I had never in our lives faced anything like this strange call from her, but knowing both of them so well and so long, we just said to Ray, okay, take care, good night. Besides, we knew the next morning we'd be in the Faithful Elders Sunday School class together, everybody playing a part—Toots making the coffee, Carol doing the treasurer's report, Ray giving the benediction. Then we'd go to the nicest place in Cadillac, O'Mealy's Cafeteria, and things might be a little stiff at the start but about the time we got to our lemon meringue pies, one of them would set things right with some off-hand explanation and nobody'd give it another thought.

On the way back home Carol and I didn't say anything. We'd both seen the big curved dent in the wall and seen Ray sitting there in his Barcalounger, rocking, even though that chair doesn't really rock, but seen him there, his head banging forward and back the way a baby will in the high chair when it's putting itself to sleep. Carol had stayed by the door, gripping the knob like she was afraid of sliding into the room. But I'd gone in and faced Ray and saw his eyes were absolutely locked on the television screen. I've never known him not to look me in the eye.

That dent in the wall was about seven feet up from the floor, just a smile there in the plasterboard like someone raised something curved and heavy above his head and swung accidentally into the wall behind himself. Also I had the impression there was something missing from the room. I looked around but couldn't figure what it was in the few minutes we were there.

Ray is a big man, as you know. We played football together at Cadillac High, and he was a good tackle, no head for strategy, not a big picture guy, but you tell Ray where to be, who to hit, and he'd do it. Many were the opponents who didn't get up any too fast after old Ray took them out. But he'd never hurt anybody off the field.

Anyway, we got home and turned in, still not talking, but just before Carol slipped out her partial, she said, "Well, are you going to say what you think of that dent in the wall?"

"Beats me," I said. I watched while she creamed her face and hands, but those were the only words spoken, and the question of the dent stood like a stranger in the room. It was the same as when you're lying there trying to hear a thief in your house. You hear a thump and picture him standing behind the living room drapes, muddy boots sticking out at the bottom. You hear a creak and think he's opening the silver drawer in the hutch. Or maybe in the silence he's sneaking down the hall to put a bullet in your heart. Bam. One red hole in the pocket of your pajamas. Bam. One red hole between the pink flowers on your wife's nightgown. You wait. You strain to listen. A pipe knocks, the furnace kicks in. You wait, maybe holding hands, maybe too scared to reach for the icy fingers you need to grip. You wait until she or you falls asleep and the other takes that as a sign and drops off too.

That's how Carol and I lay there—not moving—the same stuff in both our heads, so there was no use in saying:

But we didn't see Toots.

But she always goes to bed before the news.

But she was the one who called and yelled for us to come.

But Ray would never lay a finger on her.

We lay there saying all this in our heads, knowing what the other would answer no matter which one of us asked the question.

How could friends go off and leave a scene like that?

But it seemed all over by the time we got there.

But we didn't see her, and she'd sounded frantic.

She was probably embarrassed.

Or dead.

I was thinking it. Carol was thinking it. We should get up and put on our clothes and drive the six blocks back to check on Toots. On the other hand, in the morning everything was bound to get sorted out at Sunday School.

Everyone agrees Toots is a case. You saw her at the

picnic last year, so you know she doesn't mind setting up a fuss anytime things don't suit her. Carol and I are always glad to change seats or tables or restaurants, do anything, so Toots gets what she wants and lays off telling Ray how poorly he's managed everything. A typical example happened Saturday night.

When we were on the way to drop them off after the movie, Toots got wound up about something Ray said about what she was wearing. I only mention this detail so you can make your own judgment, but the upshot of what he'd said was that something about her dress reminded him of Shirley Temple, and she said he was calling her childish and started hitting him with her pocket book, and he hunkered down there in the back seat of our Fairlane like an old dog. You know the way a dog'll do when it feels guilty. You can't abuse it enough that it won't take every blow and come up to lick your hand and beg forgiveness. Ray was like that with Toots. Carol and I just kept laughing, the way we always did. Toots was like an angry humming bird laying into a mangy old buffalo. They're usually lots of fun, but this time Ray was whispering, Stop it! Stop it! kinda desperate like a junior high kid about to cry because the big guys are tossing his cap back and forth.

The next morning Ray was there, a big jar of Nescafé in his hand, the paper bag and grocery slip from the Jiffy right on the table the Faithful Elders Class uses for coffee every Sunday morning. Toots wasn't there. It was 9:45.

Usually by that time she had the 40-cupper perking, the glass sugar bowl full and the jar of Cremora laid out with wooden stirrers. Ray was spooning coffee into the cups with his left hand and holding the big church kettle in his right. He looked up at me like I'd caught him with his hand in the collection plate.

"Toots sick this morning?" I asked.

"Yep," he said, "I'm subbing."

I left it at that. Ray's hand, holding the little plastic spoon, was shaking.

Halfway through the lesson, Carol clapped her hand over her mouth, then whispered, "Toot's Chinese Empress." And sure enough that's what had been missing from their living room Saturday night, a turquoise and gold ceramic lamp in the shape of a Chinese lady standing on a brass base. It always stood on top of the television.

After Sunday School we usually skip church so as to get to the cafeteria before the Baptists let out and the line's out the door. But Carol and I helped Ray clean up the coffee mess and then Carol asked Ray to go to church with us. By the time we got into the sanctuary, the only seats left were in the first row, so we three filed down there.

I felt a little odd. I don't know why. I've been a member of this Methodist church since I was baptized. And if I feel the Faithful Elders Class is sufficient spiritual nourishment so I don't have to sit through one of Reverend Thorpe's moldy sermons, that is nobody else's business. But there we were with nothing between us and the preacher but a couple of feet of carpet and the kneeling rail. Thorpe kept giving us strange looks. Ray was a sight—stooped and bloated like a corpse slumped in the pew. What thoughts haunted his mind, I could only guess, but it had to be a comfort to him to sit beside Carol who is so soft and so still.

Poor Reverend Thorpe, too. He seemed completely thrown off by having us three church elders on his usually bare front pew. He stumbled along, I guess trying to give us a good show while he had the chance. But Ray's body would jerk, as though from a nightmare, and then he'd look out the window like a ten-year-old hoping for escape. Carol held his hand, patting that big paw with her silky fingers.

We stood to sing the last hymn, and Thorpe came down from the pulpit to give the benediction. He wasn't more than three feet from us, and he could hardly sing for staring at Ray. Just as we began the last stanza, Thorpe reached across the railing to seize hold of Ray by the arms like to haul in a drowning man. And it did look for a moment like Ray was going to kneel at the altar. Then we were all shocked when Ray wheeled around and ran up the aisle.

By the time Carol and I got to the parking lot, Ray's big Electra was spitting gravel and rolling out onto Main Street. We jumped in the Fairlane and tore after him. She kept telling me to slow down. I don't know what I'd thought. That he was going to finish her off? or bury the body? He was inside by the time I jammed on the brakes in front of his house. We tore up the steps. "Ray!" I hollered.

"Ray?" Carol called, sweet, but no nonsense. We knocked, and then I took hold of Carol's hand, and we waited in the glaring sun.

Nobody came. "Ray!" we suddenly yelled together. The door opened slowly and there in the shadow stood a woman I recognized after a moment to be Toots in her old housecoat.

"Toots, hon?" Carol found her voice first. "We've been so worried about you."

Toots stood, staring to the side so we could see only half her face. She looked tiny, poor little thing, no more scrawny than before, but slowed way down. If she was injured I couldn't see it there in the dim light, but I could hear her hollow breathing. I had to lean on the door jamb and stare at the threshold, so as not to feel dizzy finding this husk of someone I knew well. We stood for one more moment before it was clear she wasn't going to ask us in.

"We were wondering if you wanted to go to O'Mealy's with us," Carol said.

"No," Toots whispered. "Thanks."

"You know, Toots, by the time you dress and we get over there, the line'll be down," I offered, but she didn't say anything.

"Would you like just me to stay a while?" Carol asked. I could see Toots breathing big, but all we got was a tiny turn of her head, no.

"Well, okay," Carol said, "we'll be checking on you later."

Of course, we couldn't go to the cafeteria without them. Right then I'd have had to guess we wouldn't ever go to O'Mealy's again.

After we got out of our church clothes, Carol made some tuna salad. I told her I wanted to put mine in a sandwich and take it out in the backyard to the picnic table. She said fine, but she'd stay in the air conditioning.

I made my sandwich and took some paper towel to wipe off the table, but I felt funny, sitting out there in the sun by myself with the bees circling 'round. I don't think we ever ate Sunday dinner apart before, even if it was only tuna salad. The heat and the bees and the smell of tuna were making me sick. It felt like somebody had died. It just caved me in to think about Ray and Toots over at their house, tiptoeing around each other, completely flung off track. I caught Carol looking out the window above the kitchen sink, and I squinted. The screen darkened her face, so it was hard to make out her expression, hard to know what she was thinking.

§

Hillary O'Brian's
Cadillac Voices

This writer takes on those who put on airs about their family's Oklahoma past.

GENTLEMAN?

I'd just like to say a word or two about a certain kind of Cadillac "gentleman." I won't name any names, but they will know who they are. I call a person like I'm talking about, "Uncle Alphonse." And you may know a few yourself.

I hear this type telling new people that they come from one of the "old families" of Oklahoma, descended from the founders. Shoot! Who wasn't. Oklahoma didn't become a state until 1907.

Sure, our folks were here—living in a sod house, keeping warm burning buffalo chips. Yet Alphonse will call his relatives cattlemen, just because they owned some cows. And any one of his ancestors who went to the normal schools that trained teenagers to become teachers, Alphonse will call Scholars.

What happened to those early settlers after

that break-neck wagon race was a lot of spir-
it-crushing work and sickness that weeded out
some of the folks like Alphonse who can't call
things by their right names.

We laugh and look down on Alphonse. We
know he's weak, trying to lift himself up
backwards, painting in a made-up past instead
of working toward a better future. In Oklahoma we want you to know just how dirt poor
we started out, so you can appreciate how far
we've come. Who wants to be seen as some
namby-pamby fancy pants in a state full of
cowboys!

Sam Slocum
Cadillac resident since 1965

DON'T TURN AROUND
2013

"Don't turn around! I have a gun," I said and watched my husband of forty-two years place a shaky hand on the hutch to steady himself. I'd come up behind him. He probably thought I was still down at church. His hearing isn't all that great these days. Mine either.

This is how we always do it. While I run down and do the altar flowers, he sits as long as he wants over his breakfast. He says a man who keeps a store six days a week shouldn't have to rush on Sundays. He dresses, and then I dash back from doing the flowers to dress, and we go to church together. Afterwards we go to the cafeteria, so I don't have to cook on Sundays. We worked this out years ago. We also go where he wants on vacation one year and where I want the next. We have a schedule so we avoid running into each other in the one bathroom. It's what marriage is.

Clarence, hands still up, wasn't moving. "Barb?" His voice was hardly recognizable. I thought I'd been kidding about the gun, but some sort of authority had crept into my voice that kept my husband from turning around. Amazing. Did he feel guilty about something, expecting one day I'd catch him? Hogwash! Thoughts of his skimming from the collection plate or having a sweetie on the side were out of the question, though somehow those thoughts were thrilling to me right now—us having a showdown over Clarence's sins, me about to become a wild-eyed picture on the front page of *The Courier*—Crime of Passion. But I knew Clarence was guilt free. It was me who felt desperate. Not desperate for money or love. Just desperate. A busting out feeling in my chest. A sense of being a danger to myself.

"Tell me something, Clarence."

"What, what?" He sounded like he was about to cry.

"Tell me your heart's desire." What was I saying? Heart's desires were for kids. But I waited to see what he'd say. "Come on. Spit it out!"

"All— All my life," Clarence began and rested his hand back on the hutch, "I wanted to be a singer." He paused now, his shoulders rising and falling with the effort to get this out. "In a nightclub where the audience is real close, and I could talk to them and sing for them, and they could sing along sometimes or make requests. Just me and the audience in a small dark room, together, singing."

Good grief! Not being drinkers, we didn't go to nightclubs. Clarence was tone deaf besides. That's why I always insisted we sit on the front pew, so there'd be no one in front of him to hear him braying his soul out. I hated the thought of his wanting to be a singer. It was embarrassing. He never would have said this to my face.

"What is your heart's desire?" he asked, still not turning around.

"I haven't got a heart's desire," I blurted. Did he think this was a game? This was over.

"Ah, sure you do," he said, more in his old tone of voice.

My heart was pounding. This felt dangerous.

"Just say it," he said.

"I wish—I wish I had a gun," I said, and he jerked with laughter. I laughed too.

But already I was dreading the time when this craziness would have dried up into a joke, something so thin and meaningless he would tell friends, "Did I tell you about the time my wife pulled a gun on me." No! We mustn't ever talk about this. No one would believe it anyway. It was about as likely as our car veering off the road into another dimension.

"I guess I can turn around now, since you don't—?" he began.

"No!"

"But I've got to get dressed. Can't show up at Grace Way Baptist in my p.j.'s."

"You're going to make a joke of this aren't you? The rest of our lives you're going to be asking me if I'm armed. Aren't you?"

He turned around slowly. "You could tell it," he said softly. "Tell how at the point of a gun you forced your

147

poor husband to confess his unattainable dream. I think what we have here is a draw." He made a little smile.

"I guess," I said. I wanted to shoot us both. "We're gonna forget this, right?"

"Why would we want to forget this, the most thrilling moment I've had in ages?"

"You can't sing in nightclubs."

"But I could sing for you," he said, arms reaching as though he were singing. "We could stick candles in wine bottles the way they do at the Italian place."

"We are Baptists. We don't have any wine bottles."

After Sunday dinner I walked slowly across the parking lot. Clarence had marched ahead as usual to open up the car and start the A/C. I couldn't do this—live with a man with an unattainable dream. It would be like a virus that lived in his system and flared up unexpectedly like malaria. I wanted him to tell me he'd just made it up about the nightclub just to get my goat. But I knew it was true, and I felt uneasy just knowing it—like a crack in my life through which any kind of cockamamie stuff might creep in.

Had I always known about this side of Clarence? I broke into a sweat and stopped to lift my arm against the blazing sun. I understood now, his awkwardness, fighting that desire to open his arms and sway with the music. He'd lived his life holding that down, not swaggering when he walked, not breaking into song. And he would have gone on, successfully defeating those urges if it hadn't been for my stupid, imaginary gun.

I saw him now, leaned back against the car, his arms folded, hat pushed back like a kid with his first jalopy. He was grinning at me like I had a camera. Oh, mercy!

§

Hillary O'Brian's
Cadillac Voices

This seasoned citizen sheds a fresh light on family traditions.

FAMILY

You know around here, really, there are just two kinds of families. Those who know they got troubles and might even tell you about them if you asked. These people always shock me with their let-it-all-hang-out attitude. Talking outside the home was taboo for us. But I guess the talkers are better off than my folks, who pasted over the bad things like they could get finished with the past if they could just sell us, their own children, on the made-up things, flimsy stories to prove how innocent and smart we were.

The problem is, told so often the pretty fib, we began to feel a little flimsy ourselves and put our shoulders to the wheel in the family business of not being who everybody else in Cadillac said we were—a whole family wrapped in layers of cellophane.

I forget how cut off I am and think joy is only

motions other people go through, leaving me ashamed even of my loneliness. People will look at me funny, after they read this, but I am old now, and I don't care.

Marcus Shane
Cadillac Resident since 1952

JAMIE-GWEN
2012

Sheriff Jake Hale sat at his usual table at the Busy Bee Cafe. He was more troubled by the events of the night before than by other cases that involved a gunshot death.

"The usual?" Murleen the waitress asked.

The sheriff nodded without taking his gaze off the worn Formica tabletop. One shot had been fired from the victim's own rifle, killing him in his bed, possibly when he was asleep. There were no signs of a fight. Jake thought the victim's fourteen-year-old daughter might have been raped, although her mother, who had been asleep with younger children in another room, said the bloody tights found in a third bedroom were from the girl's period. The girl herself refused a rape kit. The rifle Jake brought back to the station turned out to have been wiped clean of fingerprints.

The neighbor who'd called Jake said the victim was a violent man. She'd seen him in a rage throw the older daughter to the ground and "wale the tar out" of any of the kids who caught his attention. "And that useless mother — ," the neighbor had sputtered. "That oldest girl was the only real mother those children had."

Jake had told the other neighbors nothing — routine inquiry, blah, blah. So, except for the body which was on its way to the county medical examiner, it was like nothing had happened. No one was grieving. No one was complaining, insisting he catch a bad guy. The newspaper hadn't picked it up. Yet. There was only a great silence from that household.

The girl, tall and thin, who had stood in the corner of the bedroom not three feet from the body, was the real puzzle. Still as an inanimate thing, neither breathing nor appearing to have any emotion, her presence had filled the sheriff with a kind of dread. And today, not able to get her out of his mind, he didn't understand at all what had happened in that house.

Jake didn't want to talk to his deputies; Curly was like a sieve when it came to spreading gossip. Fred was more discreet or maybe just didn't have any friends to talk to. If Jake had to get one involved, he'd use Fred.

The only other customer in the Busy Bee that day was Sloane Willard, a widower, who ate here occasionally, a tall, lean man who folks said had a cracker-jack legal mind. After a while Jake, who usually preferred to work out mysteries alone, stood up and walked over to the old man's table. "Mind?" the sheriff asked.

"Not at all," Willard said and folded up the newspaper spread on the table. "There isn't a lot of news in *The Courier* today anyway."

Thank God, thought Jake. "You're a lawyer, Mr. Willard."

"Retired."

"That's good, because I'd like to pick your brain and not pay for it."

They both chuckled, and Murleen brought Jake's BLT, french fries and iced tea to the table.

"Do you know the Wainwright family?" Jake asked.

"I once made a will for a grandmother by that name."

"I got a call from a woman who lives across the yard from a family named Wainwright. She said she had watched the older of the neighbor girls standing in the yard in the middle of the night. The girl looked okay, so the neighbor went back to bed. A while later she heard one shot and called me. I found the victim dead in his bed from a close range shot to the heart. His own rifle had been fired. No prints on it."

"Did it look like he'd done it himself?"

"Not really. One of the victim's daughters was standing in a corner of the bedroom looking, I don't know, like nothing had happened. Vacant. Not just a teenager with no opinions, but convincingly empty."

"Did she say anything?"

"I think she's retarded or just mute."

"Did she look shaken? Were her clothes torn?"

"What she was wearing when I got there looked okay. I found a bloody pair of tights in another bedroom. Her mother said they were hers. There are other children, three younger brothers and a younger sister, age eleven or twelve."

"What was the older girl's name?"

"Hyphenated." Jake fished the notepad out of his hip pocket. "Jamie-Gwen."

"There's nothing wrong with that girl," the lawyer said. "She was the heir to the grandmother's will. The grandmother brought her to my office. She was only about seven then, clearly smart and happy as could be about what her grandmother was doing for her, the only one of those children the woman left anything to. The grandmother had very little. She said she was going to 'put it all on the fastest pony.'"

Mr. Willard had finished his lunch and Jake gave the second half of his sandwich to Murleen to wrap up so he could take it with him.

"Thanks, Mr. Willard." Jake stood up.

"If you don't start calling me Sloane, I'll have to start billing you."

Jake drove to the Wainwright's house, a ramshackled two-story that might have been grand once but now in the light of day he could see nearly all the paint was gone, the gutter above the front door had buckled, and others were sprouting weeds. He knocked and waited. Finally Mrs. Wainwright opened the door a crack. "May I come in?" Jake asked.

"Oh no, Sheriff. I'm really not decent."

"I actually wanted to speak with your daughter, Jamie-Gwen."

"Oh, she can't talk. She's upset about her daddy."

"Mrs. Wainwright, I don't want to have to subpoena your daughter. Bring her to the door."

After an angry sigh, the woman stepped aside to reveal that her daughter had been right beside her.

"Let's talk out here," Jake said. "Mrs. Wainwright, you should join us because Jamie-Gwen is a minor."

She shut the door. The yard offered only a broken swing for seating, so Jake invited Jamie-Gwen to sit on the brick front steps. "I'm sorry for the loss of your father."

The girl said nothing. Tall and bony with dark, unwashed, tangled hair, she sat on the step, knees up, angular as a stork, her thin dress sliding up her thighs. Her vacant gaze focused on the crumbling brick walk in front of her.

"Until your mother comes out, I can't really interview you."

The girl didn't move and Jake could feel her growing even more remote. "So where are you in school?"

Not a peep. Jake looked at the girl's long hands, nails chewed to the quick, but no other hints that anything unusual might have happened to her last night. Jake looked up into the bright sunshine. Above their head in an ancient willow, birds chirped like the world wasn't dark and ugly down here.

"She's not coming," the girl whispered.

"Why not?"

"She doesn't—" The girl continued to stare at the brick. Finally she said, "—participate."

"Does your family have a lawyer they prefer?"

Jake could see the girl's shoulders rise with an inhale, but she said nothing.

Jake didn't want to arrest her, at least not until he got the forensics on those bloody tights which he'd sent, along with the body, to the medical examiner.

When Jake got home he called Sloane Willard. "What kind of law did you practice?"

"Oh, I was your legal jack-of-all-trades—estates, civil, criminal. Cadillac was small when I started out. My name used to be scrawled on plenty of jailhouse walls around the county."

"I think Jamie-Gwen Wainwright may have shot her father after he raped her."

"Really?" Old Willard sucked air. "How old is she now?"

"Fourteen."

"Hell. Oklahoma's new Youthful Offender law says if the charge is murder one, a fourteen-year-old suspect has to be tried as an adult. But you know that."

"Yeah." Jake made a dry cough. "You're not my lawyer, but I hope you'll keep a confidence."

"Go on."

"I've been thinking about this case. And I'm going to keep on thinking about it. But right now I sure would like to call this a suicide."

"I don't think you can do that. I assume you've already sent the body to the coroner. His report will be part of the public record. You better wait and see what comes back."

"Yeah." Jake was a little embarrassed now that he'd told Willard this. But goddammit. Things looked clear. That mother was too irresponsible to have rid the world of the beast who may have been raping that girl for years. So the girl, who the neighbor said, had raised those younger kids, just took the job on herself.

Neither man said anything for a moment and Jake wondered what the old guy was thinking. Then the lawyer broke the silence. "I looked at that will after we talked at noon. The grandmother left some trinkets and a little over two thousand dollars. That's not going to pay for a defense."

Hillary O'Brian, who used to cover school board meetings and Girl Scout cookie sales for *The Courier* was ambitious enough to have steadily watched the court docket and broke the story of a fourteen-year-old girl being arrested in a murder case. The defendant's name was not printed in the paper because she was a minor, but the forensic findings in the blood on the tights were detailed. The blood type was B positive, and DNA testing found semen that belonged to the father.

The town was electrified by the lurid details and some quickly made up their minds. O'Brian's articles printed comments from interviews with various citizens: "No fourteen-year-old child should be tried as an adult." "The teenagers in this town are out of control." "This was probably a Mexican family." "Thank heaven we have capital punishment in this state." "If this girl gets executed, I'm moving to New Mexico." "Men are beasts."

A week after their first meeting, Jake saw Sloane again at the café. He walked over and sat down in the booth where Sloane was eating supper. Sloane gave him a nod.

"I've arrested Jamie-Gwen."

Sloane nodded again.

"I want you to defend her. Pro bono."

"All right."

His mission accomplished, Jake knew he could stand up, but he didn't. They sat quietly for a minute before Jake said, "Maybe sometime I could buy you a beer. Or whatever you drink. Sometime at your conven—"

"How about now?" Sloane unfolded his long thin body from the booth, and the men adjourned to Antoine's, the only classy bar in town. Jake went to the bar and brought back two single malt scotches. The racket from a table full of Cadillac's wealthy, young drinkers, the Gavin McCalls included, drove Sloane and Jake across the crowded room to a quiet corner, where they sat in leather armchairs.

"Got anyone particular in your life?" Sloane asked.

"Shit," said Jake, "You get right down to it."

"I'm old. I can't waste time."

"Naw, no one. My prospects in life right now are not all that attractive to women."

Neither man with anyone to go home to, they talked on in the slow way men can who take a sip when they need to think about what they're going to say. Sloane's granddaddy had fought in the First World War, "the war to end all war, they called it," Sloane said. There was no need for Jake to say anything about how impossible that idea seemed now.

Judianne McCall left the loud table and stood now, alone at the bar. Jake watched her, a tiny redhead whose flying hair hung about her like a cloud emblazoned by sunset. Jake gazed at her until she left the bar. Then Jake turned back to Sloane who raised his wiry, white eyebrows.

The court's crowded docket allowed six months to pass after Jake arrested Jamie-Gwen Wainwright, whom the judge had allowed to wait at home. The intensity of public chatter, argument and speculation had only increased, pushing aside coverage of the town green story. Jake avoided O'Brian, the reporter. The fact is, he avoided anyone who wanted to talk about the coming trial.

The Courier reported that Judge Garner would hear arguments by the defense for a change of venue, but no one except the defense wanted that. Not the prosecutor, not the judge, and certainly not the public. A television news team had already made reservations at the Ramada Inn on the edge of town.

Sure enough there was a problem assembling a jury of nine Cadillac citizens who had not already made up their minds about Jamie-Gwen. It took eleven days of sifting through droves of people called to jury duty, and after the group was impounded, one man, liked by both the prosecution and the defense because he had been out of the country, had a heart attack. So one of the alternates would now have a vote when the jury retired to make up their minds.

During this period Jake and Sloane met several nights a week in the room back of the sheriff's office at the police station, where Jake kept a bottle. Both were uneasy about the way the jury turned out. "Too many men. Too many old people," Sloane said. "All the candidates between 30 and 60 found ways to shirk."

Jake nodded. Even though the judge had explained that elderly people were not compelled to serve, eight of the jury members were over 70, and the other four and one of the alternates looked like high school kids, although Jake knew they had to be at least 18. What he and Sloane wanted were some wise, seasoned, seekers of justice who could come to common ground and vote not guilty. This group, the gray hairs and the cell phone junkies, would not even speak the same language.

"What do you know about that other alternate?" Jake asked.

Sloane shrugged. "Schoolteacher. Church of God. Can't tell. Sometimes you can watch a juror, see if they're nodding or wincing."

"Did you know my father, Richard Hale?" Jake had wanted to ask this ever since he'd got to know Sloane.

"I certainly did. I was wondering if you were Richard's boy. You look like him. Richard Hale was a man who could stand toe to toe, outgunned, in public meetings, and speak his mind."

"Yeah, that got him in trouble." Jake tried to laugh. "Folks said he was a socialist."

"Of course they did. He was trying to organize his fellow workers at the brickworks. Anyone with sympathy for the working man was suspected of being a pinko. Folks like to forget the '50's, the communist witch hunts, the university professors who lost their jobs. McCarthyism streamed like a poison into this state. Your dad was very young then, a man with the courage of his convictions. What happened to him when he ran for the state legislature was a crime."

"Yeah, about that." Jake frowned. "When I was a teenager, I asked him how come he lost his job as foreman at the brickworks. He just said, politics."

"Yeah. What a mess. It was the fear of unions by the electric company and other—" Sloane paused now, maybe trying to remember. Jake waited. Sloane's silence wasn't like the eerie emptiness of Jamie-Gwen. Sloane was still present in friendly kind of quiet. Then, as suddenly as he had hushed, he went on. "All the big corporations were afraid of unions. Because of the loud propaganda they put out, unions became connected with communism in the minds of the public and the minds of workers themselves. The offense mounted against your dad was so virulent, it was a wonder he wasn't strung up. After the election you couldn't find a man in town who would admit to voting for him, although the vote count showed that more than a few did."

Jake's chest rose as he took this in. He remembered his dad, dead now of lung cancer, as remote. Strong, sure, but so quiet as to seem unavailable to his only kid. But this picture of a fighter for the working man, a guy with the stones to run for the legislature, this was worth everything.

"Yeah, your dad was the sort of candidate who didn't just want to be someone, he wanted to do something."

His cell phone set on vibrate, Jake sat in the back of the courtroom to hear the opening arguments. The prosecutor, Leroy Flowers, rose first and calmly presented the evidence of a revenge killing. A slender, well-made man whose white hair and expensive-looking gray summer suit gave him more sobriety than he deserved in Jake's opinion.

"The defendant, though young, acted with malice aforethought," Flowers began in a clear voice, educated, yet familiar as an Oklahoman. "This means that there was clear intent as witnessed by the neighbor who saw the defendant standing in the yard after the alleged rape and before she returned to the house to take out and load her sleeping father's rifle and shoot him in the heart.

"Malice aforethought is a time-honored legal term which distinguishes between those crimes of passion which can occur in the heat of the moment, and those which are calculated and cold-blooded, those in which a weapon is procured and loaded. In this case for revenge of a real or imagined offense.

"As to the defendant's age, a fourteen-year-old girl is much more mature than a boy of the same age. We all have witnessed girls who are more mature physically, more mature emotionally and more mature socially. Think of Jamie-Gwen Wainwright as a woman because she acted as a woman, taking justice into her own hands.

Making a plan and carrying it out. She didn't go to the authorities and report abuse. She didn't allow the wheels of justice to begin turning to protect her. No. She decided, after thinking it over in the moonlight in the side yard of her house, that she would murder her father.

"She had the motive. She believed she had been abused. She had the means: her father's shotgun which he kept in the closet of his bedroom. And she had the opportunity. Her victim was asleep. Helpless. Completely vulnerable to his vengeful daughter."

Jake's phone vibrated in his pocket, and he had to leave. It looked like the alarm had gone off again at the gas company. He would ask Sloane tonight what he'd said and how things went.

Sloane walked down from his big house, so his car wouldn't be recognized. Jake opened the back door to the police station for him.

"Why don't we just meet at the Busy Bee," Sloane asked before he sat down.

After a pause, Jake said, "I guess we could."

"But we're not doing that, are we," Sloane said.

"I know. I was the arresting officer," Jake said. "I will be called as a witness tomorrow morning. I will just say my piece, On the night of, *et cetera*. But you are the lawyer for the defense. I guess our colluding is a little strange. But is it illegal?"

"In the past, when I've wondered if something was legal, I'd ask myself, 'Would you want to read about this in *The Courier*?'"

"We're meeting because we both sympathize with this girl," Jake said.

"But that's not going to help her, is it," Sloane said. "Besides, we're meeting because we share a sense of the irony of this case. Let's knock it off."

Jake heaved a sigh. "Okay. But before you go, tell me what you said this morning in your opening argument."

"I always try to nip in the bud whatever the prosecutor has said in his opening statement. So when I got up, I said, Jamie-Gwen may be mature for her age, but it wasn't the maturity of a Jezebel; it was the maturity of the oldest daughter who sees early on that she must assert herself to care for and defend the younger children."

"That sounds good."

"I'm glad to hear you say that because that, is the kernel of my defense. Everyone I've talked to at her school and in the neighborhood believes she had been abused for years. Isn't that interesting? Not one of them reached out to her, not her teacher who saw her fading and listless, not the school nurse who saw her bruises, not the neighbors who looked the other way. I'm pretty sure that Jamie-Gwen wasn't defending herself. She'd already lost that battle with her father on the floor or in the bed or wherever he liked to jump her."

"Right," Jake said. "She was defending her family, her younger sister and her little brothers."

"Yes, they all show signs of being beaten, according to the school nurse who I will call as a witness. I've hired a psychologist as well. This wasn't so much revenge as it was a girl looking ahead, knowing that those little ones had about as much as they could take from that violent man."

"So you're not going to claim she didn't do it?"

"There's a bind with that defense. If I claim she didn't do it, what do I do with the evidence of rape? It's his semen on those tights. The jury is going to see a direct cause and effect between the rape and the murder. That can't be avoided, although the prosecution will soft-pedal the rape. But the rape is a cause, not only for the shooting. It's a cause for sympathy from the jury. The burden on me is to create enough sympathy to beat a charge of first degree murder. If the jury doesn't want to go so far as to convict this girl of a capital offence, then she gets off."

Sloane stood up. "This trial isn't going to last forever." The men shook hands.

Jake knew that instead of going himself, he should have sent one of his deputies to the gas company, so he could have heard Sloane Willard's opening remarks and been able to see the man in action or maybe not doing well. The guy was old, maybe rusty. His mind did wander. Maybe Jake should have let the judge give the case to one of the young public defenders instead of stepping in like he knew what was best. It was too late now.

"State your name and title," Leroy Flowers, the District Attorney, told Jake on June 15, the first day of testimony.

"Jake Hale. Ellis County Sheriff." From the witness stand he faced Jamie-Gwen's pale, bony presence, sitting crooked behind the defense desk, her tangled hair falling over her face.

"You were the arresting officer?"

"Yes."

"What did you see when you arrived at the Wainwright residence?"

"The body of Arnold Wainwright was in bed with a gunshot wound to his chest."

"Who else was in the room when you arrived?"

"Only Jamie-Gwen Wainwright."

"And where was she in the room?"

"She was standing in a corner near the body."

"And did you get a confession from her?"

"No."

"I mean did she confess to anything in regard to what had happened that night?"

"She murmured that she had cleaned the finger-prints off the rifle."

"And did you discover that this was true."

"Yes, sir."

"How did you discover that this was true?"

"I dusted for fingerprints as soon as I got back to the police station."

"Thank you, Sheriff."

Jake was surprised and relieved that Flowers wanted so little information from him, but he was glad to get back on the job. There had been a runaway reported that morning from the Ellis County Detention Home, and there was a break-in at a liquor store to investigate as well as the usual traffic accidents and domestic disputes, so he missed the rest of the prosecution's case, which took nearly three weeks. Everyone said Flowers was taking his time, marshaling evidence, emphasizing that this girl was a loner, regarded as "weird" by her teachers and fellow students. He returned again and again to her confession about the fingerprints but hardly mentioned the evidence of rape.

Jake followed the story on television and in the paper. He and Sloane were avoiding each other by mutual agreement, and Jake missed Sloane's support.

O'Brian reported daily on the trial. One of the most irritating stories for Jake involved an interview with Mrs. Wainwright, the mother of the defendant, who stressed how important it was to be a stay-at-home mom who always insisted on tooth brushing and proper grammar. "The important thing is that I was home in case any of my children needed me. I gave up my successful career in the entertainment industry. Caring for my little ones has been my life."

"The Hell you say!" Jake crumpled up the paper.

The temperature in Cadillac stayed in the 90s during the day and the air conditioning proved inadequate to cooling the crowded courtroom. Jake was having trouble sleeping. His house near the K-Mart was air-conditioned by a rattling box in the window that he had long ago grown used to. Something else was keeping him awake. The cuckle burr stuck in his brain was the vision of Jamie-Gwen as he had seen her the night of the shooting. The dead man was covered by a quilt drawn up to his chin to cover the hole in his chest. And there was his daughter standing in the dim light of a floor lamp. Silent and empty. Any other child would have been hiding under the bed or running to her mother. How could she stand so close? Why would she?

Jake waited until 6:00 a.m. to call Sloane, who he knew was an early riser. "She didn't do it," he said as soon as Sloane answered.

"Slow down. I haven't had my coffee. What have you got?"

"The only thing she confessed to was cleaning the fingerprints off the gun. Right? She wouldn't answer anything else. So why did she volunteer this incriminating information? And the school nurse and the doctor testified that Jamie-Gwen showed the symptoms of someone who had been sexually abused for years, right? And the neighbor woman watched her in the yard, but didn't stay at the window long enough to see her go in. See? So maybe Jamie-Gwen, heard the shot and rushed in?"

"Where did you get this?"

"If Jamie-Gwen had been abused by her father before and maybe often, what was so different about that night that would make her shoot him?"

"Go on."

"I think it was the little sister."

"Who shot him? Good grief, Jake, how'm I going to prove that."

"You don't need to. Jamie-Gwen is tall. Those tights are small."

"Those things are stretchy, Jake. What on earth possessed you to come up with this?"

"It was her standing there, Sloane, standing not three feet from the bed. Why would she even want to be in the room with the body of a man she probably loathed, if not for me to see. To be there for me to arrest, so I'd be sure to get her instead of her little sister who the old guy had turned his attentions to for the first time that night."

"So you think the older girl went outside to try to figure out what to do about her sister being raped? Why couldn't Jamie-Gwen have gone in and shot him herself?"

"It's a long shot. I know. But I think if she'd done

it herself, she wouldn't have been standing there in the bedroom."

"Jesus, Jake. It's too late. This younger sister has been part of the story—Jamie-Gwen's defending the little ones. It's dangerous for any lawyer, especially a defense lawyer, to change tactics after he's begun his argument. The jury's going to say, huh? What's wrong with this old man?"

Jake didn't say anything.

"My Lord, we have closing arguments this week. The child psychologist, my best bet, is going on the stand this morning."

"The sister is Karen. She's twelve. She'd never come to trial."

"I don't know, Jake. Jamie-Gwen still won't talk. I didn't want to put her on the stand. I promised her I wouldn't put her on the stand. I've got to go."

Jake slid quietly onto the bench at the back of the courtroom. All that could be seen of the defendant were the dark tangles of her hair above the back of the chair. Sloane was standing before a witness holding out a document. The paper fluttered in his hand. Jake had seen the tremor in Sloane's hands when he first met him, but this shaking was full blown tremor, a symptom of old age everyone on the jury would recognize as a sign of infirmity in a man who was even older than they were.

"Am I correct, sir," Sloane asked in a calm, strong voice, "that this forensics report which you as medical examiner have signed, confirms that the semen on Exhibit A, the white tights, belonged to Arnold Wainwright?"

"Yes."

"Am I correct that this report attests that the blood type is B Positive?"

"Yes."

"Am I correct that B Positive is a very common blood type?"

"Yes."

"And am I correct that you did not perform a DNA test to confirm whose blood it was?"

"Yes, I didn't DNA the blood."

"And why didn't you do this further test?"

"The sheriff didn't ask for it."

Jake felt heat in his face and wondered if people were looking at him, but his chief reaction was thank God. He left the courtroom to answer his vibrating phone. When he got back Sloane had another witness on the stand.

"Dr. Alegria, as a specialist in family dynamics, at Lakeside Women's Hospital in Kansas City, would you please assist the court in understanding rape within a family."

"Certainly," the woman said and addressed the jury box. "Although every case can have its own motives and results, there are certain patterns that psychologists have observed and recorded over decades of study. In some cases the first causal act is the abdication of the mother who no longer wants her position of providing intercourse to the father."

The courtroom was absolutely silent.

"Or the mother may also be an intimidated victim of the father's violence and threats, but in a majority of cases of prolonged sexual abuse, the mother has turned a blind eye to her husband's reach for a younger and perhaps more attractive sexual object. Men have been known to rape their own daughters when the girl is as young as two months old, but more often the abuse will start before the age of eight, when the girl is still too young to know she is being abused and too frightened to defy threats of what will happen to her if she tells anyone what has happened."

Jake bit his lip. This could be the turning point in the jury's sympathy. Or the point when the jurors want to stop listening.

"This begins a pattern," the Doctor continued, "of isolation of the girl in which the father can act with impunity. The daughter suffers a deterioration of her sense of self. In some cases her self-esteem is extinguished. There are cases of fathers who will stop the abuse when the girl begins menstruating for fear of impregnating her. In other cases, the father is seeking to make the girl pregnant and forbids her to use birth control pills. These children born to – "

"Thank you, Doctor, for this background. Can you now speak to the case of Jamie-Gwen Wainwright. Have you interviewed her?"

"Yes."

Jake felt sick. He knew more than most about what went on under the calm surface of Cadillac. But he sure hadn't known what was going on at the Wainwright's house. He had arrested this fragile, haunted girl who walked ahead of him to the squad car as though she didn't want it to leave without her. Why hadn't he noticed that this was unusual behavior then.

Sloane kept getting yeses from his witness. "Would you say that Jamie-Gwen had lost her sense of self to such an extent that she would be able to sacrifice herself to save her little sister, Karen?"

The courtroom gasped.

"Yes," The Doctor said.

Right out of the blue Sloane had pitched this. Jake was amazed. But at the moment neither Sloane nor his chief witness was saying anything. Sloane was staring out one of the long windows seemingly engrossed in the fluttering Oklahoma flag. Shuffling and murmuring could be heard from the gallery. The jurors looked at each other.

Oh, God! I did this, thought Jake. I put a senile old man in charge of a young girl's life. Sloane had now turned to the defense desk where his trembling hands shifted the papers back and forth, stopping only to adjust his glasses.

"Mr. Willard?" the judge asked softly.

"I will add just one more thing," the psychologist said, taking the situation into her own hands and addressing the jury in a strong voice. "Jamie-Gwen obviously loved her little sister, Karen, age eleven. Karen had not suffered the long-term damage that Jamie-Gwen had and was probably seen by her older sister as worth a great deal. Whereas she regarded herself as worthless and would not have hesitated to sacrifice her life for her younger sister."

"One last question," Sloane said, his gaze swooping up from the desk to lock onto his expert witness. "What happens in adulthood to a girl who as a child suffered long-term sexual abuse by her father?"

"Objection!" Flowers shouted. "This psycho-babble has gone on long enough."

"I will allow it to proceed another minute," Judge Garner said.

"They are more likely," the psychologist continued, "to make marriages to abusive men. And they are more likely to commit suicide or to go into prostitution."

"Prostitution?" Sloane exclaimed, "Why would that be, Dr. Alegria?"

"Pimps know an abused girl when they see one. If

they offer the promise of affection or just the tiniest bit of appreciation—one compliment will do—the pimp can make a prostitute of her overnight, a kind of slavery in which he will keep her overworked and afraid, a condition she had grown used to in her own home. Rarely will she be able to escape, chiefly because she does not believe herself worth saving."

"Thank you, Doctor." Sloane turned to the Judge. "Your honor, this was my last witness."

The judge looked at his watch and said there was plenty of time this afternoon for closing arguments. He asked the two attorneys if they were prepared. They both said yes. "This is Friday. After I charge the jury, they can retire and deliberate over the weekend. Or as long as they need."

As in so many trials Jake had witnessed, the verdict hung on one detail: Did Jamie-Gwen go back into her house before the shot was fired that killed her father as Leroy Flowers promoted, or after the shot was fired, as Sloane Willard had strongly implied. That was the weekend's work ahead for the jury.

"So, Boss," Jake's deputy Curly asked, "have you got any money on the verdict?"

"No." Jake was trying to have lunch alone at The Busy Bee.

"You know that lawyer with the glass house?

What's his name?

"McCall," Jake said, not looking up. "Gavin McCall."

"Whatever. He said Flowers has an open and shut case. He said juries like hard evidence—forensics, confessions, ballistics. A lot of blather by a psychologist won't cut it with juries." Curly was standing on one foot and then the other beside Jake's table, appearing not to realize that Jake didn't care about the opinions of Gavin McCall and kept his head down eating his BLT. "Of course," Curly continued, "McCall may be sore at women 'cause his wife left him."

Jake put down his sandwich and looked up. "Judianne McCall has left her husband?"

On Monday evening, just as darkness fell on Cadillac, the jury brought back a verdict of not guilty. When the jurors were interviewed, O'Brian was jostled aside by a full rank of television cameras, photographers and reporters from across the state. The yard was packed with excited members of the public talking about the verdict. The jurors who wanted to speak stepped in front of the cameras and had a lot to say about the responsibility of holding a girl's life in their hands. More than one of the young jurors made selfies with an arm around the neck of the old lawyer who several said, "Took the heat off us by giving us reasonable doubt."

Jake stood on the edge of the crowd as Sloane entered the bright spotlight to speak to the press and the mass of the public. The old man blinked and adjusted his glasses. Then, in full voice and without notes called out across the crowd. "Keep your eyes open, folks." The crowd hushed. "Don't turn a blind eye on the kid who sits alone in the park. Don't pretend not to see that blank-eyed girl who looks so shabby because she feels so un-loved. Reach out to those loners whose hurt is so deep they push you away." Then his gaze grew more intent and his voice stronger: "Don't give up on the young and vulnerable who may quietly suffer savagery at home!"

Sloane stepped out of the bright light and craned his neck to search the crowd. When he spotted Jake, he nodded and walked his way.

§

Hillary O'Brian's
Cadillac Voices

The Courier *is pleased to have received this colorful piece from a member of our valued academic community.*

THE LAND RUN

Who among us here today would have the courage or the skills to line up for that harum, scarum race, the Oklahoma Territory Land Run of 1889? I know some of you are descendants of the brave souls and adventurers in wagons, buckboards, buggies, train cars, horseback, bicycles or on foot who made the first land run into Oklahoma Territory's thousands of square miles of treeless land and endless days of sunshine. A farmer's dream.

Of course, in hindsight we are aware that those treeless plains, parching sun and the plow combined to produce the dust bowl forty years later. But at the time, for those land-hungry pioneers, land was free, people were friendly, and hard work was going to guarantee success.

Penniless immigrants, as well as folks who owned marble topped tables and swallow-tailed coats, lived in dugouts and sod houses until wagons could haul in enough lumber from Texas and the state of Washington for proper homes. Anybody too proud to live in a sod house had better scoot on back East where a sissy could keep his fingernails clean. Right?

The sodbusters could thrive, and salary men do the clerking, but the Oklahomans who got rich were the high-rolling risk-takers who had luck, willfulness and the stomach to gamble. After oil was discovered in 1919, a Harvard degree wouldn't get you a cup of coffee, no siree, but any roughneck working in the oil fields figured all he needed was land on a lucky spot to become rich. And this dream became for us both our myth and our expectation.

Stan McCurry, PhD
Cadillac Community College
History Department
Cadillac resident since 1996

SUGAR HOUSE
2010

The Sugar House used to be a real tavern over on old Route 283 — one of them places with four stools and a jukebox. It's got a big oak rocking chair now for me, but it used to be a place to buy beer and hang out. You wouldn't want your girls over there, but you'd hope your boys chose it over a lot worse places.

Well, this whole tiny honky-tonk was lifted up onto a flat bed truck and brought over and set down on a new slab right here in the trees at the edge of Cadillac's Juvenile Detention Center. Every child when he's growing up needs to go across the tracks to the bad side of town once in a while. Here at the Center, that's what the Sugar House is, a runned-down place to sneak off to and pretend you're not a child.

Now if that surprises you, let me tell you something else — that it was a lawyer that did it — Sloane Willard bought the place himself and plunked it down here twenty years ago and sent me to be the cook when I was about to be sent to the penitentiary.

I guess this isn't going to make any sense unless I go on and tell you that I killed my husband. Shot him in the neck with his own rifle. Mr. Willard, my lawyer, said it was a crime of passion because of the awful fight that was going on at our place, but between you and me, it felt like cold blood.

I'm big, some say fat, but I'm as strong as any man in this whole institution even if I am an older woman. There are folks who will be afraid of someone as big as me, my own kids were, I'm ashamed to say, especially Ronnie, the oldest, who caught the worst of it.

I used to try to tell the details of my husband's killing so folks wouldn't be afraid of me, but I quit that. My pastor at Graceway got me to stop. He was real young then and kinda odd, talked more like one of the psychiatrists around here than a Baptist minister should. He said, "Lena, forgive yourself." That sounded real strange to me 'cause in those days I was stark ravin' crazy hoping God and the children would forgive me for killing their daddy. They'd all been screaming—Ronnie and my oldest girl trying to help me, and the little ones too scared to move. 'Course afterwards they were all hanging on me and telling me it was okay, but I knew they'd never forget what they saw. And sure 'nuf, when I'd go to whup one of them, I'd see the fear in their eyes.

Now you're wondering what happens to the six kids of a woman who shoots her husband. Mr. Willard had known my family when we all lived in Ardmore. It was him suggested to the judge she send all my kids to the Juvenile Detention Center and send me and the Sugar House along too. My kids and me had our own cottage, and they went to school with the rest of the kids. They're grown up now, pretty much okay, law abiding.

Here at the Detention Center we mostly get your incorrigibles—chronic truants, runaways, boys who've been selling theirselves to buy drugs—kids whose folks have turned them over to the state to raise. There's more of that than you think, sometimes rich kids—thirteen or fourteen years old whose folks have given up on them—broken-hearted little cusses who feel totally evil. Like this new kid who came in last night except he was only eleven or twelve—dark straight hair, small for his age, still had baby-soft pink cheeks. He had a big expensive leather jacket slung around his little shoulders. I'd been told in staff meeting that we had a hard case named Stephen, but this was his first time to come my way.

He sat all hunched over with his head down on one of the back tables away from the music and the counter, almost out of my sight, 'cept nothing is really out of my sight 'cause that's how the Sugar House is made—one big room where I can serve snacks and keep an eye out for the hard cases. When I see this kid come in, I go over and say, "What'll it be," and he gives me and a couple kids that's playing checkers real mean looks.

I've seen this look before. I call it feeling swampy—feeling all dark and snaky inside, like something that creeps along in the ooze, the worst, most loveless thing God made. And I'm smart enough to know when a kid is feeling swampy, he'll strike out—stab you with a pencil or an ice pick if he can get it. And this little guy was like that.

After awhile he raises his head and starts trying to gouge a hole in that old table with one of them plastic spoons. Well, I know he's doing that so's someone will say, 'Quit that.' So I go right back there and say, "Quit that, kid. That ain't no sand pile. How about digging into some ice cream, instead." What does this little hard case do but ups and turns the table over—would have hit my toes if I hadn't jumped back. He's standing there with his hands on his hips trying to look tough. The leather jacket on the floor.

"Stephen, you put that table back the way you found it."

"No, you old bitch," he says so loud that the other kids get up and leave, probably embarrassed 'cause they've known me a long time or maybe just giving me room.

"Now listen," I says, "we don't talk that way here, and nobody tears up the Sugar House."

"Oh, yeah," he says and reaches behind him and rips the old Michael Jackson poster off the wall.

"Yeah," I say. Then before I know it that kid scoots across the floor like greased lightning and slides behind the counter. He grabs a Pepsi bottle out of the rack, smashes it on the sink, and holds it up like he's the bad guy in some gangster movie. Well, I been here twenty years. This kid and his jagged bottle ain't

185

nothing new to me. But he wasn't crying, and his eyes looked kind of frozen.

I sit down real slow in my rocker like I'm taking my place in the pew at church. I know violence. It's got three mean triggers: Fear and rage and pain, any one will blast out and fire up the other two. The only thing to stop it in yourself is to fling your mind out somewhere's else, and he don't know how to do that. So, sitting there in the rocker, I commence real serious-like to study a hangnail on my little finger. He's standing there wielding the bottle at nobody and trying to keep up his fierceness, and I say, not looking his way, "Did you ever go to a rodeo?"

"Everybody's been to a rodeo, stupid!"

"Yeah, I suppose you're right."

"This isn't a real place, it is?" he asks.

"You mean the Sugar House?"

"It isn't really away, is it? It's part of the prison."

"That's right," I say. "Yonder through those black jacks, you can see Cadillac's water tower through a chain link fence when the leaves is all off in the fall.

"I hate you," he says, and that bottle is flying right in my face. I duck and come up to see him yanking the cord out of my toaster. I jump up so fast I turn over a table. The toaster's on the floor, the plug's still in the wall, and he's holding the cord with two wires hanging out. And what he does next like to paralyzes me. He opens his mouth and starts to stick the wires in.

"No!" I scream and reach across the counter to yank the cord out the wall. He runs out from behind, but I grab him around the middle, pinning his arms to his sides. He's kicking like the dickens.

"Lemme go, lemme go!" he screams.

"No!" I flip him up so's I got him like a baby, the legs up against me with one arm and his top half with the other, and he's pitching like an alligator, but I hold on and carry him over to the rocking chair. He's screaming bitch and old cow and a lot of other stuff, and I sit down with that bucking creature in my lap.

"I hate you!" he screams. "You are the biggest, fattest bitch I ever saw."

"Old Dan Tucker was a fine old man,
Washed his face in a fryin' pan."

I begin to sing and bounce my knee in time just to wear him out.

"Combed his hair with a wagon wheel
And died with a toothache in his heel."

Then I start really bouncing big, letting fly with the old knee so's I'm bucking more than he is.

"Get out the way for Old Dan Tucker

He's too late to get his supper.
Supper's over and the dishes washed
and nothing's left but a piece of squash."

Well, we go through about six rounds of this—me singing "Dan Tucker" and bouncing my knee and him screaming dirty names and trying to get loose. Finally he slows down, exhausted, but I don't let go because I know like any landed fish he's got a few leaps left in him. So I switch over to "Yankee Doodle," still bouncing some, still acting like we're fighting. He's feeling pretty heavy now, and by the time I get to "O Susanna" the poor thing is more dead than alive, and we're both soaked with sweat.

"What do you want to hear?" I jiggle him like I'm trying to keep him awake. "How about 'Jesus Loves me'?" I say.

"I hate it," he says

"Well, I love it, so you're going to hear it," and I start in with "Jesus loves me, this I know..." and I'm singing and looking him right in the eye and he's looking back like he's seeing a crazy woman.

This poor creature in my arms ain't got nothin' inside to lift his heart, and he's a dead weight in my arms. So I do "How Great Thou Art," to pick me up. After that, "He Leadeth Me" and then, my grandmother's favorite:

"I come to the garden alone,

While the dew is still on the roses."

That one always makes me cry because I think of her and how she poured out her heart trying to make up for all that was missing in my life. And I cry thinking of my boy, Ronnie.

The hard case is lying still, a great big boy with his legs hanging down, and his wet face against my shoulder. I sing real soft now.

"Abide with me
Fast falls the eventide."

Stephen sniffles and right as I'm closing down says, "Know what?"

"What, Stephen?"

"I never got to see a rodeo."

"Aw, that's a shame."

Then he gives one last shuddery little sigh and closes his eyes, me still holding onto him, singing, same way as I hold on to myself.

§

Hillary O'Brian's
Cadillac Voices

We are very fortunate to have as our Voice this week, the Editor-in-Chief of The Cadillac Courier, *Mr. Eliot Tarman, who writes some startling news about the history of Cadillac's founding.*

AN UNFORTUNATE DISCOVERY

The city of Cadillac has long been proud of its name, which has a connection to Detroit, Michigan, but nothing to do with the luxury car. It was our innocent belief that we were founded by a direct descendent of Sieur Antoine di la Mothe Cadilac, (1658-1730) a French fur trader, colonial administrator in America and the founder of the city of Detroit.

Duane Will in his book, Oklahoma Towns, (Oklahoma University Press, 1985), had part of the story right:

CADILLAC, OKLAHOMA. Established in 1832 by Pierre Cadillac, the first postmaster in what is presently Ellis County. Located on the Butterfield Overland Mail route prior to the Civil War. In 1854 the name was changed to Okolona from the Choctaw word oka lobali, meaning "a place caved in or washed out by water," but changed back to Cadillac in 1858.

But I'm sorry to tell you, *Courier* readers, that was not the whole story. Dr. William Normand Little in his History of Oklahoma, 1800 to 1940, (University of Oklahoma Press, 1953), casts a cloud on the founder of Cadillac who claimed to be a direct descendent of that famous fur trader. Dr. Little writes, "Pierre Cadillac may have emigrated from Canada in 1829, arriving in Indian Territory in 1831 or 1832 . . . . According to letters written by citizens of Cadillac in the 1840's, Pierre Cadillac's name originally was Abner Spottle. Neither French nor famous. Sorry folks.

Eliot Tarman
Cadillac resident since 1972

Mother said if Minnie and Uncle Sloane could get anything out of it at their ages, it was okay with her if they lived together. But mother's cousin Marvella said it was an insult to the memory of their spouses, and Minnie should, at least, drop out of the Bible Club until the matter was settled.

This all came up in the winter I turned twelve. I had been listening for years and knew this was not the first time in our family that a widower had decided to take in his widowed sister-in-law to keep house for him, and if the first case created a scandal, no one brought back word to us in Cadillac. I think they were mostly old folks in that little town, and old folks are sometimes more practical than younger adults like Marvella, who are scared that elderly persons might become sexually revived and benefit themselves at the expense of the family reputation.

I saw this fear fueling Cousin Marvella to tear out of my mother's kitchen that winter morning to go get everyone straightened out. Now my mother wouldn't criticize Marvella any more than she'd criticize Sloane or Minnie, but she did say, as Marvella was fighting her way into her fur-collared coat, "Perhaps we ought to let them sort this out themselves."

"Alice, you know this sort of thing can just ruin a family. It's almost, well—" she glared at me. "You know," she whispered to Mother, "it's almost incestuous."

"Well—" Mother bit her lip. "He's always welcome to eat over here, but with all these children I don't have time to take stuff over to his place. And neither do you. So maybe—"

"Then he should hire a cook." Marvella swept out, leaving the door open.

"I think that's what he's doing, in a way," Mother called after her, then closed the door and rubbed her arms to warm up. She looked at me a little sheepishly. "Phoebe," she said, "I'm sorry you had to hear all this."

In about thirty minutes Marvella called to say that Sloane hadn't even let her take her coat off at his place, and she was going to start the papers to get him declared incompetent. Mother said Marvella should sleep on that idea. Then mother made a couple of calls to Sloane and Minnie to invite them to dinner.

"What are the chances of you two getting married?" my father asked after we'd all finished our salads and started on the ham. I knew mother had put him up to this. Dad never had any ideas about people on his own.

"Zero," Minnie said and pushed out her lower jaw just a tad, then went back to her green beans.

Minnie always seemed especially happy to be in our family, although I thought she'd married the dullest of the lot—Uncle Bob, one of Sloane's older half brothers.

Mother had been the first one Minnie told about how glad she'd be with the new setup. She'd be getting out of her nephew's place and having Sloane's range to cook on. This particular appliance had a double oven with a light in both and a deep-well cooker which fitted down into one of the top burners. Minnie's prune face was not one that could be said to light up, but I could tell she was crazy in love with that electric range.

She did plain cooking, plain housekeeping, and gave peculiarly practical presents to children at Christmas time, the kind of gifts we opened while trying not to look disappointed. My three-year-old twin sisters once got rubber doilies to paste on the bottom of the bathtub to keep bathers from slipping. I received a new toothbrush and dental floss.

After getting Minnie's quick negative to Dad's suggestion about a marriage, we all looked at Sloane. Even in his 80's, he had style. Legend said he'd put himself through college and law school playing cards for money. Since his retirement from practicing law, he'd followed state politics and had closely reasoned opinions about the collusion of some churches and the Republicans. That's what he called it, collusion.

Other than his staring spells, Sloane's only failing seemed to be a sort of sloughing of the generations. More than half the time he called me by my mother's name, which I didn't mind since she was his favorite niece. With my mother this time lapse took a more peculiar form. He would sometimes take a dime from his pocket, place it in her palm, fold her fingers over it, then kiss her on the forehead.

We were all waiting to get Sloane's answer to Dad's question. Sloane seemed to be trying to read something off the grapes on the wallpaper. Finally, under the pressure of our stares he said, "Please pass the yams."

Dad looked at Mom for help.

"Oh, it was just a thought," she said, smoothing her damask napkin, taking full responsibility for the unpopular suggestion.

Sloane put down his fork and rested his long fingers on the table edge. "Perhaps, if we found Marvella another husband," he said, "we'd be acting more to the point." Then he gave me a sidelong glance, and his bristly eyebrows shot up as though he'd just made a joke.

That night in bed, I listened across the hall as usual, and I heard Mother say, "Herb, I think he's half doing this just to get Marvella's goat."

"Well, he'd better be careful," Dad said, "because as the child of his only full brother, she's his next of kin, and she could make real trouble."

She did, of course. Everyone in the family began to get stiffer and talk less and less, at least to us kids. All I could find out was that Sloane had to go to court to prove he wasn't insane. That little dent between mother's eyebrows appeared, and it stayed there.

"Can I go to court?" I asked Sloane three days before the big day. He was settling down with the funnies after Sunday dinner. Mother had already said no.

"Why Phoebe, I was counting on you to sit with me," he said, smiling, the only one who hadn't stiffened up.

"Mother said court wasn't a place for children," I said.

"She's right, of course. Leave them home—just you and Herb and Alice come."

I remember thinking, it was magnificent being twelve.

Some of the older women in the family were in an agony of shame over Uncle Sloane's impending sanity hearing—not of course so much the suggestion that a member of our family was possibly insane, something we had faced before, but the real shame came from the nature of the evidence against him, his deciding to have Minnie live with him without benefit of wedlock. Two of my father's unmarried aunts left town to stay in Enid with their widowed sister until this embarrassing episode passed.

Minnie herself, was not, however, of this delicate constitution and showed up in court that morning wearing a new poncho she had crocheted herself.

Sloane looked quite handsome in a dark blue pinstriped suit and polka-dotted tie. He and I sat with his lawyer, Horace Medberry, on the front bench. Dad came up and hunched down in front of us. "Now Sloane, you understand what we're here for?"

Sloane looked down at my father.

"This is a hearing before that judge up there." Dad pointed to the front of the courtroom

"I know that's a judge, Herb. I've been in court before."

"Well, Alice and I just wanted all this to be fresh in your mind."

Uncle Sloane looked toward where Marvella and her lawyer sat. They were talking with Alfred Truitt, our family doctor. Dad then gave another worried look at Horace Medberry, Sloane's lawyer and lifelong friend, who sat quietly dozing on the other side of Sloane. Dad went back to sit with Mother.

I noticed that Sheriff Jake Hale was standing against the wall at the back of the courtroom. This made me anxious that he was there to escort Uncle Sloane to the state hospital when this was over.

We all waited a while longer for the judge to stop conferring with the bailiff. Nobody said anything except at one point Sloane slapped the bench we sat on and said, "Oak." Then he stretched to the side to put his hand in his pants pocket. "You want something for the collection plate?"

"No, sir," I said.

The judge called the hearing to order and asked Dr. Truitt to speak first.

He allowed as how he'd known Sloane Willard and

his family all his life and had been his doctor for almost fifty years. He kept darting looks at my mother. I turned to see her sitting with her hands clasped on her knees and her mouth pursed.

"Do you find Mr. Willard's judgment competent to lead his own affairs?" the judge asked.

"All I know is, he has spells."

"What kind of spells?"

"Spells of inattention, confusion."

Marvella began to mutter: "The poor old man is 82 years old and losing his mind! You've seen it happen." She glared at the doctor. "Tell him!" she whispered, but we all could hear.

Judge Saunders cleared his throat and asked, "Do you believe Mr. Willard is sufficiently impaired to need care in the state hospital?"

Dr. Truitt folded his arms and looked at Marvella. He took a breath like he was about to say something, then stood up, and I thought he would make a speech. But without being dismissed, Dr. Truitt squeaked open the door to the witness box and walked out of the courtroom. The judge watched him go as though it weren't any of his business where the prime witness in this case was off to. There was a murmur in the court and Marvella herself stood up and pointed at the doctor as he walked out the door, jabbing her finger in the air as though to show the judge what was happening. The judge called Minnie to the stand.

"State your name?"

"Minnie Willard."

"And your age is?" the judge asked.

"Sixty-five," Minnie said.

Mother rolled her eyes.

"And what is your part in all this?" the judge asked Minnie. She blinked and jerked her head back and forth in her clucky hen way. "Why, I am the sister-in-law, the housekeeper. I thought you knew that!"

"Yes, I know, but what do you expect to get out of all this?"

"I expect to get out of my nephew's house. His wife is the worst—" And Minnie was off on the subject of the woman's housekeeping. Before she could get to the part about the electric range, the judge got her turned off and called Uncle Sloane to the stand.

I place my hand on the bible, say "I do so swear," and sit down in the witness chair. But this is all backwards. I should be standing, pacing back and forth in front of the judge, defending my client. Where is my client? I can hear the judge saying, "Mr. Willard, would you tell us your side of things?" But there is little to say except, I have suffered great losses.

I gaze out at the almost empty courtroom. Margaret? There she sits in the back, our boy beside her. Her shiny hair is swept back from her wise brow, her smile warm as sunshine. I could use your help, dear wife. But then they are gone. Losses. Maybe the young are scarred more deeply by loss, but it is the old who stagger under the weight of its accumulation.

"Uncle Sloane! The judge is talking to you." It is Marvella, my niece.

I turn toward the judge. "I'm 82, your honor."

Marvella reared up. "You see, your honor, you see. I am trying to save the poor old man from himself!"

"Sit down, Marvella." I sounded like a tired parent.

"You can't talk to me like that," she said.

"I'm sorry, your honor, Marvella is my brother's child. I'm afraid she's cross today."

The judge blinked and leaned up on his elbows to speak softly to me. "And what, Mr. Willard, would you say has made her cross?"

"Why sir," I said, "I suspect it's because she's embarrassed about my domestic plans and believes all our lives would benefit from her having power of attorney. Perhaps you and I could agree that I'll put a little notice in *The Courier* saying Marvella Ketcham should not be held responsible for the arrangements at Sloane Willard's house."

Judge Saunders clicked his gavel and said this case was dismissed. Marvella set up an awful fuss, but the judge ignored her and invited me and Horace to walk down to the hotel for lunch. Jake waved from the back and gave me a thumbs up. I invited him to join us, but as usual Jake had to go back to work. Minnie said she had to go pack if she was going to move in time to cook supper, so I asked Herb and Alice if they'd drop her at her nephew's place.

With a faint smile Alice said, "I guess we're out of the woods for awhile, Uncle Sloane."

Phoebe looked puzzled. "Uncle Sloane, what really happened?"

§

Hillary O'Brian's Cadillac Voices

There has been very little criticism of the Homestead Act which peopled Oklahoma with hard-working farmers and others seeking their own plot of land. That may be because the lot of women was rarely mentioned.

WIND

They say the wind drove my great grandmother mad. But I know the wind alone won't do it. A woman had to be lonely first, cut off from the folks she left in Nebraska or Pennsylvania. She had to have a dream for the future—a tow-headed child sitting at a spinet, his music lit by a lamp with a hand-painted globe. That would do it.

Let her carry that vision with her into the dugout. Let her call upon that picture as she pulls the tarp around her and her children, huddled like animals in the ground. Let her cling to the box that holds the tiny pins for Latin and Elocution. Let her remember rose water and Sunday School picnics with angel food and strawberries her mother cultivated back of the cistern.

Let her hold these images as she stands on a dry prairie she cannot see the end of, forty miles from the nearest church. That would do it.

They tell me in Europe the farmers used to put their rakes on their shoulders and go into their fields in bands, returning at sunset to the village. Their women shared the well, the oven, the comfort of laughing together at the men. But my great grandmother, thanks to the Homestead Act, floated alone within violent oceans of land.

Hazel Matlock
Cadillac resident since 1954

COUSINS

My cousin, Veronica Jane, is that sort of thirteen-year-old person who thinks she's a cheerleader even though she definitely is not. She's got a mother who is a great shopper, so all her clothes fit just right and look new, and she puts this little twist in her walk that flips her skirts and gives the impression that she's going steady with someone over at Cadillac High although she definitely is not. I know.

She says things like, "Guess where I got this" — some stupid little charm her daddy gave her. And "Guess who I was with Saturday night" — even when she was just at Grams with her folks watching Wheel of Fortune. How dumb does she think I am?

The worst happened last Christmas when Gram gave her some little white drum major boots and a baton. This was absolutely pointless because Cadillac Junior High doesn't even have a marching band. But Little Miss Cutie Pie was in ecstasy — picking up her feet and stomping 'em down in those white boots like she was down at O.U. or something. It was the coldest Christmas Oklahoma had had in thirty years. So we couldn't play outside, and all we got all over Gram's house was boot stomping and hip twisting. Gram gave me a quilted bathrobe, and said it made me look like Jessica Lange. But everyone just went right ahead watching the baton girl. It was right after Christmas that I began to leave the notes.

The first ones were nothing—just little experiments—a line or two poked into her locker: HI YA CUTIE. I made it look crude and heavy like boy's writing and used plain white paper from the art room.

Veronica Jane is not bright. She has the body of a mosquito, but the brain of a gnat. There was no problem fooling her. Last period she has gym, and I'm upstairs in home ec near the lockers.

She showed me the first few notes when we walked home. Our houses are less than a block apart.

"Oh, goodness," I said the first time. "Are you going to tell your Mom?"

"Maybe, maybe not," she said kind of sing-songy, wagging her chin and shoulders and hips all at once. She said she knew who the guy was, and I begged her to tell me, so she had me where she wanted me. She thought.

I kept leaving notes three or four times a week. Then I figured things were going too smooth, so I turned up the heat a little. WHY DON'T YOU EVER SMILE AT ME? I wrote on a piece of white construction paper. We were supposed to be making skirts in home ec. But you know how that goes with 32 girls in the class—bring in a pattern and material, then stand in line to get it okayed by Mrs. Chishom. Then pin the pieces on the cloth and get in line again. Then cut it out and get in line—anyway

205

it's all stupid and takes forty times too long to make a skirt, but there's plenty of time to talk and write notes, and Mrs. Chishom will let anyone go anywhere during class just to get rid of a few. Sharon Black once got a bathroom pass and went out for a hamburger and a malt at the Jiffy and came back just as the bell rang, and naturally Mrs. Chishom just said thank you when she turned in her pass.

It was wonderful to see the way Veronica Jane began to smile at the boys last winter. I swear I saw her massaging her cheeks to get the kinks out of her sore muscles.

"Has your cousin lost her mind," Crethie Mashburn asked me, "the way she keeps sticking that smirky grin into every boy's face?"

"I hadn't noticed," I said and added, "poor little thing."

YOU, YOU ARE THE ONE, the next note said.

Veronica Jane had a little smile on her face on the way home.

"Heard from Romeo?" I asked.

"Oh, I'm getting kind of tired of those silly notes," she said. She lied.

Every Sunday after church, since time began, we all eat at Gram's. Our whole family, Veronica Jane and her folks, and Aunt Minnie, of course, who used to live with us before she moved to her brother-in-law's big place. After dinner everybody is just supposed to lie around while Gram cleans up. The men watch TV or talk about their cars, and my Mom and Aunt Malti, Veronica's mom, talk about how awful it is that Gram won't let them in the kitchen or who had on what at church or how cute Veronica Jane and I used to be when we played together as babies. Urp.

I always bring a book and try to stay out of everybody's way. But Veronica Jane just flits around the house, perching here and there like a canary getting petted by this relative and that one. Gram practically paid us to play together last year. "You're lucky to have such a sweet little cousin. When you're grown up, why, I bet you're just like sisters," she'd say to me. Then Gram would mention how Veronica Jane was an absolute double for Shirley Temple, whoever she was. To make Gram happy I tried to teach Veronica Jane to play Monopoly, but she just kept saying that this wasn't real money. Hopeless.

I forgot to leave notes for awhile, so the next one said, SORRY I HAVEN'T WRITTEN, BUT I'VE HAD TO HELP MY BROTHER FIX HIS CONVERTIBLE.

Now I knew this was getting tricky. Romeo was now the younger brother of someone who drove a convertible. That had to limit the possibilities to just two or three boys, but I went ahead and dropped it in her locker on the way to the bathroom during Chishom's class.

"He drives a convertible," she whispered.

"Who does?"

"The boy who leaves the notes."

"Oh. Has that started up again?"

"Of course. I hear from him every day. I don't tell you everything, Miss Smarty," she said staring hard at each car that passed.

"He must be pretty dumb," I said.

"Dumb. What do you mean?"

"To be old enough to drive and still be in junior high, he must have been put back at least twice."

"No, no. It's his brother's car. He wasn't put back. He drives it on the weekends."

"I hope he doesn't go to jail."

"No, no—just around their property."

"He drives round and round the house?"

"No, no, it's a big ranch. He drives around their ranch. That is perfectly legal. Isn't it?"

"Oh sure. Their own property. Not the city streets."

YOU NEVER WEAR THAT BEAUTIFUL PINK BLOUSE ANYMORE, I wrote while Chishom was checking side seams and everybody who wasn't sewing or asleep was standing in line. I took a chance and slid the note under Veronica Jane's locker door after the bell rang. This was all getting too easy.

Veronica Jane ran home as fast as her mosquito legs could carry her. I said I just couldn't keep up. There was no rush. Mother's church circle had had their rummage sale the Saturday before, and I had folded up Veronica

Jane's pink blouse myself and put a twenty-five cent sticker on it. I saw a dumpy woman from the country buy it.

I watched Veronica Jane running home to try to save that blouse and knew that this was just the beginning of the things I could make her do.

I THINK YOU'D LOOK GREAT IN PIGTAILS.

Veronica Jane's hair is kind of wispy and not very long. She does it up in pin curls every night, then fluffs it out as much as possible in the morning. I thought she'd never try braiding it, but next day, sure enough, her head looked like an onion—all those little blond wisps slicked back with water into two of the most pitiful, scraggly pigtails you ever saw.

"Your cousin looks bald," Crethie Mashburn said.

"We're all real worried about the poor little thing," I said.

We were finally getting around to hemming our skirts in home ec. It had taken an entire marking period to get all 32 zippers in and school was nearly over. I had let up on old Veronica Jane for a while and just slid in an occasional flattering note to keep her on the string while I thought of one last trick before school was out. I started hinting that Romeo wanted a date.

I'D LIKE TO SEE YOU IN THE MOONLIGHT. That sort of thing. Finally there were only three days left.

MEET ME UNDER THE HORSE APPLE TREE AT 9:00 O'CLOCK FRIDAY NIGHT.

This tree, Mother called it an Osage orange, was in the corner of the school grounds behind the football field. In the fall the big green pulpy apples fell on the ground, making a considerable slippery mess that everyone avoided. Right now they were probably just big, stupid green oranges no one could eat. I knew she'd never have the nerve to go there, but I liked the idea of her stupid Romeo picking such a gunky place.

I'd forgotten all about this and was lying on my bed Friday night reading when I heard Aunt Malti come in crying that Veronica Jane was missing. I jumped into my shoes and dashed out the back door while Mom and Dad were trying to quiet down my aunt. Believe me, I never, ever thought she'd go. I ran so fast that when I came around the edge of the bleachers I was gasping and had to stop and rest my hands on my knees. I was only a little ways from the tree and could just make her out there in the dark under the strange branches. She was facing the other way and her arms were wrapped around her like she was cold, even though it was real warm. She looked tiny, like a little child, lost. I walked toward her as quietly as I could. Suddenly she turned and when she saw me, she froze. There in the dark, like someone playing statue, she didn't move a muscle. I didn't move either.

"You!" she whispered.

"Come home now, Veronica Jane. Your folks are worried."

"You."

"Shucks, Veronica Jane. What are you talking about?"

"It was you all along."

"Look. I'm sorry."

"Sor-ry?" she whispered, her mouth and eyes wide open.

"I just—it was just—"

"Sor-ry?" she croaked and hurled one of those hard green horse apples at me. I ducked but it hit the top of my arm. She reached up to get another one.

"Wait!" I was backing up, and she was coming toward me.

"Sor-ry?" She zinged another horse apple into my hip. Wow! Like a baseball. "I hate you!" she screamed. She was out in the moonlight. I was running.

"I said I was sorry!" I turned and faced her. "You were so stupid."

"Stupid?" She ran with all her might and pushed me. I went down hard, bit my tongue and slid on the wet grass. I jumped up and faced her. She was bawling like a two-year-old now. "Don't call me stupid! Don't ever call me stupid! You think you're so smart. That's all I hear from Gram! Your grades and your brains!" She ran and slammed me down again, and before I could get up, she dropped down hard straddling my stomach. She was

211

crying and trying to pin my arms down.

"Wait," I yelled. "Gram never talks about me. It's you. You all the time—Little cutie pie!" I struggled up and pushed her off. "You spend all your time looking in the mirror. Weren't you even suspicious about the notes? Didn't you ever wonder?"

She rolled away from me and sat in the dark with her arms wrapped around her knees. "I hate you," she whispered. She looked pitiful hunched over there in the wet grass. She'd been so easy to fool.

I just sat there tasting the blood in my mouth. I spit a couple of times. It was dark now. A dog barked a block or two away, but other than that, it was real quiet there on the football field, nobody saying anything.

Finally I said, "I guess we ought to get on back. They may call the police and get Gram out of bed, and then she'll have a heart attack."

"Let her, the old battle ax." Veronica Jane said through her teeth. I was surprised. I didn't know she had it in her to say something like that.

"Yeah, I know," I said.

She looked surprised now. "I thought you were her—"

"Her favorite? Naw, that was always you."

Finally she got up and came over and pulled me up. I smoothed down her hair, and she had a look at where the horse apple hit my arm. Then we walked slowly around the football field once, taking our own sweet time, before we started back.

I kept thinking about next year. Eighth grade was going to be hard for her — science and math. Kids can be so mean.

§

Hillary O'Brian's
Cadillac Voices

I ran across this old clipping in the archives of The Cadillac Transcript, *the paper that preceded* The Courier, *and noticed some familiar family names. Older residents might find their grandfathers here.*

FROM THE ARCHIVES

May 15, 1917, Cadillac, OK Sunday afternoon almost every citizen of Cadillac turned out at the depot to bid farewell to seven Cadillac High School seniors who enlisted in the army. Losing no time in volunteering to serve their country, the day after their graduation these boys climbed on the train for Camp Doniphan, the massive training camp set up on Ft. Sill to assemble, house and train our boys before they ship out for Europe. Mayor Wills, a veteran of the War Between the States, made a speech congratulating the boys on entering "the glorious tradition of taking up arms in defense of liberty." The high school band played "Yankee Doodle" and the Methodist Women's Circle threw rose petals on these, our next heroes.

Less than three months after our President

declared war on Germany, these young men and hundreds of others throughout all the counties in Oklahoma have valiantly joined the forces of what President Wilson called the "war to end all war."

"I figure the Germans asked for it," Wilbur Bagby, one of the volunteers was quoted, referring to the marauding German submarines that have begun to attack our ships along the merchant routes between the United States and Great Britain.

"Them Krauts won't have a chance. All us are sure shots," said Carl Heiligman. "I'm itching to get me a uniform," he added.

Sloane Benjamin Willard was asked why he was volunteering. "I can't let my friends go off without me. They might get into trouble." He grinned, and indeed there was a smile on every face at the depot.

FIRST MOVE

For Beatrice, the summer session at Cadillac Community College had a ragged ending. She'd been sitting alone in Dr. Devlyn's classroom for nearly forty minutes, wearing her student look—jeans and a sweater, her hair pulled to the back of her neck in a rubber band—trying to decide whether to stick her head in his office to ask him to sign a copy of his new book. This should have been easy for her, a well-fixed widow with lots of social skills. She thought she could approach anyone. She looked again at her watch.

Suddenly, tall and grave, he stood in the doorway. "Mrs. Patterson?"

"Oh, Dr. Devlyn." He had a narrow face and soft gray eyes. Not taking her eyes off him, she reached into her bag.

"Is there something I can do for you?" he asked.

She swallowed and half stood, blocked by the desk arm, her hand still in the bag, gripping her copy of *The Singing Heart*. He reached out to catch the tipping desk chair, which hung now against her lap and the back of her legs, making her a stooped, six-legged creature. She let the book drop back into the bag. "No. Thank you, though," she said and sat slowly, letting the chair legs back onto the floor. What is wrong with you? she asked herself.

He dropped his arms to his sides. "In that case—" He shrugged and made an awkward step backward. She had decided he'd probably married young before he developed any easy ways with women, then was divorced and marooned here in Cadillac, trapped without instructions on how to break out of his wrapper.

She sat a long time letting her breathing calm and her cheeks cool, as his spirit slowly faded from the room. What was going on? She used to have everything under control. Her mother put a lot of stock in that—sitting properly, knees together, keeping your opinions, if you had any, to yourself. "The worst thing a woman can do," Mother used to say, "is to embarrass her husband." Beatrice had buried Harold, having never embarrassed him during their twenty years together. Nor had she encumbered him with the details of her life. In twenty years had he ever looked closely at her?

The course, Nineteenth Century Women Poets, was over. She took out Dr. Devlyn's book and opened to the first page.

The first flakes of snow drifting out of the gray New Hampshire sky commenced a winter-long sadness in Anna Robie. Eventually the snow would cover the stony pastures and fill in the rutted roads, cutting her North

Country family off from town and church and neighbors. Winter, which she once called "that brutal king," forced her "eyes into the gorge." And yet it was in winter, exhibiting all the signs of chronic desperation, that Anna Robie produced her most profound and lyric work.

The last two classes of the course had been devoted to Anna Robie, whose poems, diagonally inscribed across the pages of an almanac in a tiny squarish hand, had only recently been discovered in an Orford, New Hampshire, farmhouse. The new owner of the house had passed the almanac on to his friend, Sam Devlyn.

A contemporary of Emily Dickinson, Anna Robie had encoded in lyric blank verse the harsh details of drunkenness, violence, longing, and death. Dr. Devlyn created a seamless fabric of interviews, town records, agricultural and weather data, interwoven with the poems themselves. He had discovered that Anna had one year of school at Amherst Academy in Massachusetts before returning to New Hampshire to marry at age eighteen. He wrote that the sixteen poems grouped under the title, "Suspension of Life," were written between the death of a baby son in January 1842—a year of record cold according to other diaries—and the May thaw, when the Robies dug the infant grave found among other tiny markers surrounding Anna's stone.

Dr. Devlyn said his book wasn't a real biography, just a glimpse from the distance. But, oh, Beatrice marveled at the attention with which he brought from total darkness into a gentle candlelight the life of this woman, born 1812 and, after bearing nine children, dead in childbirth at age 38. Beatrice had read the book through in a weekend, and when in the dark hours of a Sunday morning she got to the last page, she flipped back to start over, not wanting to break the spell of bleak beauty. How could he, a man, know this long dead woman so intimately? What drew him to the details of Anna Robie's life—the curve of her knife around the apple, the blue shadow of death beneath her children's eyes, her fear that loneliness would freeze her heart?

Beatrice snapped the book shut. Dr. Devlyn wasn't teaching the fall semester. She'd lost her chance. She slipped *The Singing Heart* into her bag, walked out and closed the door behind her. As she passed the Dean's Office, she could see Marge, the receptionist, smoothing lotion up and down her wrinkly arms. Marge had straightened out Beatrice's summer school schedule last June, and Beatrice had begun to confide in her. Beatrice laid these lapses in her usual restraint to being a schoolgirl in blue jeans three days a week. She stopped in the doorway.

Marge squinted at her. "Hard final, huh?"

"We didn't have one."

"So why are you looking so washed out? Don't tell me you didn't get the book signed." Marge frowned. "Look, just give a party if you want to get to know him. You look real good, and I know you must have a nice house. Just be casual."

"He wouldn't want to go to a party," Beatrice answered. "The book was my only excuse to approach him."

"That's what's wrong with you. You think you need an excuse. I knew you were a lady the minute you walked in here in June. Don't your friends tell you that?"

Beatrice let her bag slip to the floor and sank into the plastic chair in front of Marge's desk. No, her friends never talked to her like this.

"Look, Beatrice—" Marge leaned across her desk and whispered. "This Dr. Devlyn may have completely petrified, living out there in the country so long. He may have a PhD from State and some publications, but his books aren't the kind that really make a career—too poetic, not enough footnotes. Forget this guy. There's a new botanist coming in next semester."

Beatrice lifted her bag to her shoulder. "Maybe I should just drop by his house and ask him to sign it."

"Oh? A house call, huh," Marge said, "That's not casual."

"Being casual wouldn't do this man justice! What is his address?"

"Don't snap at me. I'm just saying, it's not your style."

Four days later she guided the car onto the shoulder of the section line beside Dr. Devlyn's ordinary white rural mailbox, its red flag down. The house was a small ranch style, set back maybe a hundred feet from the road. She'd passed by before. Because of the ditch along the road, the only approach to the house would be to walk up the driveway. His car, all the shine scoured off by the sandy wind, was parked in front of the garage.

She put her hands in her lap and stared through the windshield. There were no trees on this road, just waving grass, one neighbor's mailbox a quarter mile on down and then the horizon. The sun was sinking into a band of purple which stretched above a strip of pale greenish blue just above the earth's edge. She mustn't arrive after dark. That would be forward.

She turned off the engine. The racket of crickets sprang up around the car. She rolled down the window then wrapped her arms over the top of the steering wheel. The odor of baled hay was on the breeze. She'd lived all her life in this county. Maybe a thousand people in town and in the Methodist Church would say they knew her. She touched the book. He'd read a long passage in class, a poem about pulling turnips in the cold wind, the rough stems against work-tortured fingers. His rapt attention to each word made her grit her teeth against a pang in her jaw.

The sun had slid beneath the purple band and now shimmered, a liquid orange pressing the black earth. There were only a few minutes before dusk. She started up the drive, but stopped. Marge was right. This wasn't her style. She stepped onto the low porch, knocked, and held the book against her pounding heart.

The door opened almost immediately. "Yes?" He leaned forward to see her through the screen of the aluminum storm door. It was dark behind him.

"I failed to ask you to sign the book the other day, then I found out you weren't teach—"

"Mrs. Patterson?" He pushed the screened door open, and she could see him—tall and serious in jeans, his shirttail out. He was barefoot. In the orange light of dusk his narrow face looked older, deeply etched. She had never stood this close.

She stepped forward, putting her shoulder against the weight of the screened door's spring. "You were a wonderful teacher," she said and swallowed hard. He looked down at her with a mild squint. Angry? Embarrassed? He didn't invite her in. She'd made a mistake, put herself in Anna Robie's place, felt understood and attended to. "You seemed to care so much about her."

"Robie? Yes, I did."

"It made me think you—"

"Really? You thought I—"

"I thought you could read women."

"No. I have a bad record on that. I don't even try to read live women. Not anymore. I'm sorry. I preached a lot of intimate insight about a woman who wasn't present to straighten me out. Look, my house is a wreck. I can't ask you in. I'm glad to sign the book. Is that what you wanted?"

Beatrice stood very still and waited.

Finally, he took in a long breath. "You drove all the way out here, so I guess what you really wanted—" He paused squinting at her.

She said nothing. She was a grown up. She could do this, stand toe to toe and wait. It was dusk now on the prairie.

"So I guess you wanted company." He was nodding, encouraging himself. "You wanted my company." He was studying her, taking her in.

"Do you want to go get a root beer?" she asked

He nodded again. "Let me get my shoes."

§

Hillary O'Brian's
Cadillac Voices

The clipping from the old Transcript about the boys joining up for WWI touched a lot of people, who sent in interesting historical details about their families as well as sorrowful accounts of grief and loss. This piece is from the descendant of three generations of veterans.

CIVILIAN

My great grandfather, a soldier in WWI, married a volunteer nurse he met in an army hospital. Their only son was my grandfather who fought in WWII and came back to the University of Oklahoma where he married the girl who had waited for him. Bobby, their only son, my father, went to Vietnam when I was two. He didn't come back.

We are a thin line, a sapling of a family tree of which I carry the sole remaining seed. Reading that clipping from the old newspaper made me think about war and children.

I am 38, unmarried and childless. I have not served my country, and am now too old to do so. I want to find a wife; I want to be a father, but I haven't the luck to find the right woman, or to have ever met the kind of woman who would wait four years for me while I huddled in rainy fox holes on the other side of the world.

Our family luck began to sputter when my father was taken prisoner by the Viet Cong. My mother once told me, knowing he was a prisoner was worse for her than finding out later he was dead.

She watches me out of the corner of her eye. She asks me how I'm doing. She never asks me, "Where are my grandchildren?"

Gene Hunter
Cadillac resident since 1975

AS TRUE AS ANYTHING

Behind the kitchen here at Marvin's Truck stop, there's a small room where we used to throw broken tables and chairs and store the cases of beer. About ten years ago a prostitute ran a lively business back there until the highway patrol cruised in and took her away, so last year I was surprised to see a little Asian gal moving in a high table and a lot of white sheets. Marvin told me she was a masseuse, and she showed up every Monday night around 9:00.

Offering massages to truck drivers seemed odd and risky. If she was a whore, the smokies would soon sniff her out, and if she was offering real massage for your health, then why was she coming out here instead of staying in the nice place, Cadillac Nails & Spa, where she worked in town? Marvin, who was always thinking of ways to bring in more business, said she'd come to him and they had made a deal.

I'd taken her for Vietnamese, there being a lot of them now, but she told Marvin she was from the Philippines, had married an airman at Clark Air Force Base maybe twenty years ago and moved to the U.S. when he transferred to Tinker Field. I got the feeling she'd left him in Midwest City and moved here. She was a hit with the truckers—some detouring down from Kansas. I could

226

have come up with the $20 for 30 minutes but I didn't want to give up the way my mind imagined it. Her name was Rose.

My name is Sonny Higgins. I'm the dishwasher at Marvin's, and except for a few wins in the rodeo spaced out over my lifetime and some jobs not worth mentioning, my resume is pretty thin. It's not like bull riding and breaking horses prepares you for much in later life except bar fights, and even that's more than I can handle these days. My back is still strong, but one of my shoulders rides a little higher than the other, and I'm stiff pretty much all over. The good-looking bronc riders, no matter how broken down, can marry well-off widows who maybe have a trailer and a government check, but the rest of us wash dishes or pump gas.

I worried about Rose and kept my ear cocked in case she yelled for help. And sure enough, a few weeks after she'd started, a local guy came bulling in, drunk as a skunk, swearing about how he was "gonna fuck her good." There was a big crowd that night, plenty of beer on the floor and smoke in the air. This bastard almost knocked over old Veronica, who was carrying a tray of burgers, then he paid no mind to the guys waiting in line. I tripped him as he came charging through the kitchen, and he fell and cracked his head on the sink. He was out cold and I threw him over my shoulder. Marvin and I got him back into his car. Our policy is, by the time a guy figures out Marvin's got his keys, he's sober enough to drive.

Rose came and stood behind me at the end of the night. I wanted her to place a healing hand on my shoulder, but she didn't. Her sweet little voice said, "Thank you, Sonny." I didn't turn around, just nodded and said sure. Hell, she didn't need me to protect her. She was getting famous. Truckers don't have anything to do but talk to each other on their cell phones. And more than this, being near the door to the storeroom, I could tell she really knew what she was doing 'cause every Monday night I'd hear little bits of what was said with each new guy. "Have you had any recent surgery? Are there any injuries I should know about?" And I'd picture her sitting on the folding chair in her jeans and a shirt like the nurses wear in the emergency room, and him, sitting there on the edge of the table, buck-naked, clutching a sheet around himself. You should hear those truckers go on. She never stops them, just lets them run down then says, "Okay, I'll turn around and you lie down and fix the sheet over you." A guy who has just reported the details of the worst accident he was ever in or what his dad did to him when he was twelve isn't gonna give any trouble to the woman whose hands are comforting him. But still, I worried about her.

Hoping to get a woman's point of view, I asked Old Veronica what she thought about us having a masseuse at Marvin's and was surprised that all she did was pull in her chins and say, "She's okay." I'd thought maybe Veronica, with those ropey veins behind her knees and the arthritis in her hands, would be jealous and say something sarcastic about the younger woman.

"Do you think she'd let me buy her a cup of coffee?" I blurted.

"Don't be a sucker, Sonny."

One night I decided to fry Rose some eggs while she was gathering up the dirty sheets. It was about 2:00 a.m., and the cook was out back smoking, so I had the stove to myself. I leaned on the pass-through, watching the top of her head while she ate. She had long straight, glossy black hair. Her feet barely touched the floor under the counter stool. She had broad shoulders and big hands for her size but they didn't keep her from looking like a kid. Her skin was the color of old piano keys, but there wasn't a line on her face, and she had a child's sweet smile.

My cooking something for her before she left got to be a weekly thing, and one cold, snowy night I slid the plate in front of her on the counter and poured us both a cup of coffee. I'd known her for six months, so I sat down beside her and she didn't seem to mind. "So, Rose, how'd you get into this line of work?"

She sighed like she was too tired to talk, but she said, "My father was a trucker. Had a route from Manila through the mountains north to Sarrat. He supported eleven of us."

"Gee."

"When he came home at the end of his route, he'd lie on the floor and I'd sit on his back and rub his neck and shoulders. Truckers lead very unhealthy lives," she said, then stopped to eat a little. I sipped my coffee and waited until she took it up again, talking easy, the way I'd hoped she would. "They smoke. They sleep in the truck. They lift heavy loads. Too many hours. The noise. Terrible posture."

"Sure."

"They're overweight. No balanced diet. They self-medicate—way too many narcotics and analgesics and antihistamines. Then they get ringing in their ears, high blood pressure, ulcers, hemorrhoids—"

I was getting sorry I'd brought this up.

"He died in his forties."

"I'm sorry."

"It was a long time ago," she said, but I could see she was still angry about his health.

"So you got into this 'cause you took pity on the truckers."

"And they've got no health insurance, and in 20% of crashes the driver fell asleep."

"Is that what happened, he fell asleep at the wheel?"

"No." She thanked me for the eggs and took off into

the snow.

Rose's list of what was wrong with truck drivers made me think about the deterioration of men from their work. And I mark that night as the beginning of looking hard at myself, beyond the physical damage and asking myself what I had to offer as a man. I was decent, whatever that meant, but did I have courage? Maybe I was just bull-headed the way my mother had always said I was. Go ahead and climb on that wild horse, you damn fool! I can still hear her.

I knew how to comb my hair and put on a clean shirt and sweeten up my breath, but all that seemed superficial and temporary. I lay awake nights pondering all this and wondered how her dad died and why she wouldn't tell me. My life went on this way until I realized that Rose was all I thought about and all in this world I wanted.

I carried on cooking for her every Monday night and sat beside her while she ate, but she seemed to drift farther away from me and talked less and less. At first I laid it to being winter, when some people get grumpy, but it got harder to hang on to any hope of getting to know her because she gave me no encouragement but a muttered thanks.

One night when the place was packed with truckers waiting out a rainstorm, I could tell she was really low. She had plenty of business, and though she looked completely beat, she didn't even sit down, just took one look at the eggs and toast and walked out in a way that made me think that was it. She wasn't coming back to a place where she had to eat supper with the dishwasher. It was a mighty long week for me, waiting for the next Monday to see if she'd show.

But she did drag in. Whatever was on her mind had her bent like an old lady. I stuck to business, no eggs, just kept my hands in the sink.

Around 2:00 in the morning she came up behind me so quiet, I jumped. "I need some help moving," she said.

My stomach went cold, and I whipped around to face her. "You're leaving?"

"No, just a new place."

I bucked up with the idea that I would see her place, and I didn't say anything and may have looked a little goofy as I was picturing myself carrying a huge couch on my back with no help from anyone.

"There's not that much stuff," she said, as though I'd been stalling.

"No, no. Course not. Sure."

"When are you off?"

"Same as you."

"Okay, Tuesday noon. Okay?"

"Sure."

I was not surprised to see that she was very organized. Her little place was small and dark, but clean as a whistle, and she had everything except for the furniture in boxes labeled kitchen, towels, photos. In less than an hour we were done putting things in the truck she'd borrowed from her friend Tina and were rattling down the highway, me at the wheel.

After we got everything inside the new place, a sweet little duplex with lots of light, I tried to open a box labeled kitchen, but she said no and sat down on top of it, not gonna let me see her stuff. She motioned to a kitchen chair for me to sit down, but she had her arms crossed like we were about to have a fight. I made for the door. "Wait," she said, "what do I owe you?"

Nothing could have hurt more. "Not a dad-gummed thing!"

I am not a greenhorn when it comes to women, but I have shit for luck. I was married twice by the time I was twenty, first time when I was seventeen, a false alarm. Her folks handled the divorce for us. The next time lasted four years. My wife and I danced, drank, fought and followed the rodeo until one day she took off with a trick rider who had a Crown Marquis convertible. I was pissed and tried to find them, so I could, at least, knock his pretty teeth in, but honestly, I couldn't blame her; she was only twenty-one, and I already had a limp. The real truth is, she would have stayed if I'd treated her better. At the divorce I gave her everything except my horse and saddle. I took full custody of the guilt. I had girlfriends after that, but I knew I wouldn't make a good husband.

I was still standing, not knowing whether I was going or staying. Rose just sat there on the box, very straight, arms crossed, jaw clenched, looking past me out the window. The setting sun shone on her shiny black hair. I sat down in the kitchen chair.

I couldn't say I've learned much about the differences in the sexes. I get lots of time to think while I have my hands in the warm dishwater, but my schooling was brief and poor, and I don't read anything but the newspapers the truckers leave behind. I stood up again to go, feeling stupid for having had thoughts about our putting the dishes and pans away, maybe even putting the bed together and tucking in some sheets. Stupid. Stupid and insulted. I grabbed my jean jacket.

"Wait," she said so softly I barely heard it.

"What is it you want, lady?"

"More than a plate of eggs!" she said loud and clear. I'd never heard a rough word out of her before. Was she saying I hadn't been a good boyfriend. I hadn't, of course. I didn't even know when her birthday was. She was quiet again, rocking a little on the box obviously working up to something she was anxious about.

"Just spit it out," I said.

"I just don't want to be alone anymore."

I waited for her to go on and realized my mouth was open and I should say something.

"I don't want to be alone myself," I said. "What'd you have in mind?"

She tightened her grip on her ribs, pulling her T-shirt smooth against her little breasts. "I don't want to just live together, be half way all the time."

She didn't want to live together? Hell, we'd never seen a movie. My heartbeat had picked up to a steady gallop I could hear inside my head, so I couldn't think of the right thing to say. "You want us to get married?" I blurted. She bit her lip. "Sure," I said, the way I always say sure when I have no idea what I'm talking about. Get married? I didn't know. I just wanted to wash down the cabinets and put the canned goods away and roll out the rug and move the furniture around until it suited her. But something was wrong with the way things were going. "I don't get it," I said. "We're friends, but you don't really trust me, so I can't figure why you'd want us to hitch up."

"I trust you!" A big dent like a check mark appeared between her eyebrows.

"Then tell me how your dad died."

Her face kinda flared and then tightened. "No," she said. She seemed to be thinking about talking, but then she stood. "Thanks for all the help." She was expecting me to stand too, but I slouched a little further in the chair.

"I don't talk about that," she said. "Sorry."

I've never been the kind who went in for persuasion.

Either a woman wanted me or she didn't. But Rose was the one who brought up us getting together, and now she was letting all that go to hang onto some secret. I scratched my jaw. Maybe I didn't know how to be persuasive, but I sure as hell knew how to be stubborn, so I took out my pocketknife and began to scrape my fingernails.

She sat back down. "I can't tell people about my dad's— I've never told anyone."

"Not people. Just me." It was getting late. In all our rush to get everything in the house, we hadn't turned on any lights. She was completely in shadow, and I wouldn't have known she was crying if I hadn't heard her gulp for breath.

"Talk," I said softly.

"Huh uh," she sniffled.

"Rose. Talk. My life depends on this." Where that came from I didn't know, but it seemed as true as anything I'd ever said.

I heard another shuddery breath, then she leaned her elbows on her knees and said to the floor, "As he got older the run got harder and harder for him. He never went to a doctor, but I'm pretty sure he had emphysema. He smoked almost as much as he coughed. Going north was no problem, he said. He was rested from being at home. It was the way back, exhausted after unloading in Sarrat. That was the worst." Her pinched little voice got steadier.

236

"When I was sixteen, he taught me to drive and started taking me with him, showing me the route—where it was dangerous, where the police hid. I loved being away from home. This was a very easy life—just riding along with my papi, no little children to look after and no women to tell me what to do. After I got used to the route, he asked me to drive some on the way home, so he could rest." Rose glanced up, but she couldn't see me any better than I could see her. "I loved driving the truck, especially at night in the moonlight, singing softly along with the radio while my papi slept."

"One night just before my seventeenth birthday—" Her voice tensed up and I gripped the edge of the chair as she went on. "I looked over at him and saw that his seat belt wasn't fastened. I should have stopped right then and fixed it, and I told myself I would, but I just kept on singing, thinking only of myself, on top of the world, driving that truck." And then she stopped and I listened to her sob.

"That's okay," I said. "There was an accident and he died. That's enough."

"He was crushed!" Sobs shook the word out of her. "The truck rolled over," she whispered. "I never told anyone about the seat belt."

Jesus, she'd been only sixteen and had carried this for maybe twenty years. Finally I said, "Why don't you get up off that box, and we'll put the kitchen things away." I gave her a hand up and took her easy into my arms. She rested her cheek against my chest, so her tears leaked into my shirt. Holding that little thing was like a shot of morphine. I wasn't going to ask her if she was sure about me. There wasn't going to be any more serious talk tonight. After we kissed, she stepped away from the box, and I knelt down and slid my pocketknife gently through the packing tape.

§

Hillary O'Brian's
Cadillac Voices

This insightful piece was slid under The
Courier's *door over the weekend.*
Thank you, whoever you are.

FRANKNESS

I have noticed that in an Oklahoma woman
frankness is not a virtue. It counts for the same
thing as rudeness or selfishness. What gets a
great deal of credit is sweetness. In Oklahoma it is good to be sweet, whereas in the East,
I'm told, the word means stupid. Of course, if
an Oklahoma girl had her choice, she would
choose beauty, that being prized above all
else. She won't admit it, but the first thing an
Oklahoma woman will tell you about another
woman is whether she's beautiful. "Walter's
new wife isn't beautiful, but she is sweet."

But frankness is a flaw. "One always knows
where Maude stands," my mother used to
say—meaning Maude should keep her thoughts
to herself. If a lady is asked for the truth, she
should create some gossamer distraction to
waft in the face of the questioner, some veil
from which all lament has been wrung.

When I'm asked, "How are you coping since your mother-in-law moved in?" The proper answer is, "It's so handy now we have the hospital bed. When I hold the baby up, grandmother smiles at him like she knows who he is." This sort of evasion has the added advantage of discouraging friendships with frank people who might lead one into the path of self-expression.

What I must never say is what, for me, would be the First True Things: I married the wrong man. I am disappointed in my children. I am dying of loneliness. There will be no stars in my crown for blurting out such ugliness. My line is: I sure am lucky to have this lovely man and these lovely children and live in this really, really lovely big town. Over time, of course, I fear, such diaphanous puffs of meringue will cause my teeth to rot, and my daughters to despise me.

Anonymous

Just as Ellis County Sheriff Jake Hale was fishing another donut out of the bag on the floor of his patrol car, his cell phone rang. He recognized the number of the Juvenile Detention Center. "Hello, Mr. Baird," he said to the Director.

"Sheriff, we got an urgent situation," Baird wheezed into the phone.

Between Baird's mouth-breathing and the crackly cell phone the County had issued Jake, this was going to be like talking to Darth Vader. "I'm on my way," Jake shouted and shut off the phone. Likely another runaway. The place was like a sieve. And why not. It used to be the Methodist orphanage, and the security installations had never caught up with its being a holding pen for juvie felons, hard luck minor offenders, and whackos awaiting decisions from psychiatrists. He'd rousted them out of the cotton fields surrounding Cadillac and tracked them down in the lower bowels of Ellis County.

Jake speeded up, turned on the cherry, but resisted firing up the siren. Sirens just got people excited.

As he drove up the long driveway onto the detention center grounds, Melvin Baird waved to him from the high ground around the flagpole. Jake got out and waved back as Baird, thin as a rail and hunched, skidded down the slope to meet him. "Sorry to get you out so early, Sheriff, but we've got a real bad situation. A transfer has a gun."

"Yeah?" Jake took out his cell phone and speed dialed his deputies while Baird continued to talk.

"He shot a long-time employee, and he's holding a girl in the cafeteria."

"Jesus!"

"I know."

Baird pointed to the windows along the side of the cafeteria, a low building that faced across the central yard to the administration building.

"Can we see them?"

"No. At least I couldn't looking across from my office. But the boys claim he ran into the kitchen pantry off to your left."

"Any windows to that?"

"No."

Jake moved toward the end of the building out of sight from the windows. With Baird close behind him he looked sidelong inside to see the deserted tables, scattered cereal bowls, and overturned chairs. "You said there was a girl, a hostage? Where'd he get a girl around here?"

"She must have been somebody's visitor."

"So early in the morning?"

Baird took out his handkerchief and mopped his

forehead and the back of his neck. "I haven't done all the investigating I like to do when we have an incident. Interviews and so on. But the gun—"

"Where're the rest of the kids?"

"We put them with the staff in the gymnasium."

"How's the guy that got shot?"

"It was a woman. She's at the hospital. Wounded in the arm."

"Who's the kid with the gun?"

"Darrell Sturm, fifteen-year-old, male Caucasian."

"What else?"

"Sorry. He's only been here two weeks. A transfer from Custer County because of him having an uncle in Cadillac. We're trying to reach the uncle right now."

"What'd the kid do?"

"Sold drugs."

"What kind?"

"Marijuana."

"How'd he get the gun?"

Baird's hands went up like he was stopping traffic. "We have absolutely no idea. No idea. He certainly didn't have it with him when he was registered two weeks ago. And he's had no visitors. We're absolutely sure of that. The uncle hasn't shown up at all. We never have guns in here. Nothing like this has ever—"

"How many outside doors?"

"Main door on the right end and the kitchen door

around the other end."

"Loading dock?"

"No, no. You just walk right in. I wish I could tell you more about him."

The place, so deserted, could have been any school. The gym stood beyond the playing fields. The day was overcast and heavy. The rope hitch clanged against the flagpole. Jake had been on a real high last night with Judianne, that feeling of being a guy who could handle anything. He hadn't been able to imagine the right woman until he'd seen her. She was married at the time, but he'd waited for her to get out of that. But this morning that belief in their future had quickly drained into that pit he called What I Have to Offer Her. No raise in ten years. His shabby house at the edge of town, surrounded by the parking lots of K-Mart and Krispy Kreme, sank deeper into the weeds every day. He'd barely been re-elected last time. "A lightweight," his opponent called him.

"Back when I came here," Baird was saying, "our biggest problem was boys getting into fistfights. What the County sends us these days comes in worse and worse."

"I'm familiar. Who'd he shoot?"

"Lena Brandt, an aide, an elderly woman. Been here longer than I have. She's the big gal who ran the little snack house for the boys. Everybody liked her."

"Any other shots?"

"No one else has been hurt."

"I'm counting bullets."

"No other shots. As far as I know."

"You wouldn't know what kind of gun it was?" Jake asked and watched Baird's lower lip pull down. "That's okay." He glanced at his phone. "My deputies are on the way. We'll tape off the area, so we'll have control. Then I'll go in and see what I can do."

"Do you have a bullhorn?" Baird asked.

"I don't like bullhorns. You keep everybody in the gym including the staff. Don't call anyone else. If that uncle shows up, have him come to me. The best way will be the simplest. The kid's probably scared and waiting for us to get him out of this. You stay in the gym with everybody else."

As Baird worked his way toward the gym in a wobbly jog, Jake's cell phone rang. He looked at the incoming number. Oh Lord.

"Hello, Mr. Mayor. What can I do for you this morning? . . . Yeah, I'm on top of it . . . . . The Guard? Criminy, Walter. We're not going to call in the National Guard for one little guy. Besides, what's left of our boys are still in Afghanistan. How'd you find out about this situation? . . . I didn't know your niece worked here . . . . Look, if anybody else calls—" Jake looked up to see the very man he was talking to walking toward him across the yard, cell phone at his ear. Jake waited until they were face to face, and the mayor had lowered his phone, then

Jake said, "I'm hoping to handle this very quietly, Walter. And alone."

Two men in tan uniforms trotted up. "Okay, you two," Jake said, "There's a kid in the cafeteria with a gun. He may have a girl with him in the storeroom on the left end. I want yellow tape around this whole building, twenty feet out. And across the drive. Absolutely no trespassers. I don't care if the Governor shows up. Then one of you at each of the doors."

The mayor cleared his throat. "I don't need to remind you, Jake, that one person has already been shot, a county employee, no less. What's your plan?"

"My plan is to wait until the kid gets hungry and offer him a Big Mac. Okay? Now if you could just—"

"I'm staying."

The back of Jake's neck prickled. He was used to people being stubborn. Usually his size and the badge were enough. And now, over the mayor's shoulder, Jake saw a guy in white shorts and T-shirt walking toward them from the gym. Matthews, the Baptist minister.

"Hi, Sheriff, I was here for basketball practice," the reverend said. "Anything I can do?"

"You might go collect all the cell phones in the gym."

"I'm afraid it's too late for that. It seems like every member of the staff made at least twenty calls in the first ten minutes."

"Jesus! Pardon me, Reverend."

"I'll go back and see if I can calm everybody down, maybe get a constructive discussion going."

"Thanks."

Before he even turned around, a new Lincoln pulled up the drive. "Wait, Reverend Matthews, wait up!" the driver called. A trim man in Hawaiian shirt and a crown of silver curls got out and ran across the yard. He gave quick nods to Jake and Mayor Mashburn.

"Percy Pikestaff, minister at The Living God." he said to Reverend Matthews and laid his hand on the taller man's shoulder. "I'm so glad to catch you here. My wife just called me about this tragedy. I'm calling our phone tree right now. If you could get your people out, we could have a huge impact. Circle this whole building in the powerful arms of prayer."

Jake's stomach took a queasy lurch. "No! Cut that idea right now. We don't want any people here. A crowd is the last thing we need."

"This wouldn't be like a mob. These are all Christians." Pikestaff turned back to Reverend Matthews. "This is the chance of a lifetime to prove the power of prayer. Are you with me, Reverend Matthews?"

Matthews slowly shook his head. "The sheriff's right about a crowd. Besides," he raised his eyebrows, "a good deal of my congregation has already gone over to The Living God. They're probably already on your phone tree."

Pikestaff cut off a quick smile, walked up the slope to the flagpole and took out his phone.

"Shit," Jake said. "What do they believe out there at The Living God?" he asked Reverend Matthews.

"Oh, they're a mix, Baptist, Church of God, probably some Methodists. And a lot of folks who've never been to church."

"He's cutting into your congregation, huh?"

"People want to belong to something big," Reverend Matthews said, "I'll see what I can do in the gym, maybe something active, although the kids are likely too keyed up to play anything with rules."

Jake frowned at the mayor, who showed no more signs of leaving than Reverend Pikestaff had. The mayor, who was probably hoping to get his picture in the paper, just shrugged, his sport coat rising and falling beneath his big ears. Jake looked away and felt one of those damned-if-you-do, damned-if-you-don't days rising before him. The bark of a faulty muffler alerted him to the arrival of a small red pick-up. Oh hell. Where were the deputies with that yellow tape? Jake ran toward the truck hoping to reach it before the small woman in blue jeans and flying red hair got out of the cab. The mayor followed.

"Christ Amighty, Judianne," Jake whispered, leaning down beside the door of the truck. "What the hell are you doing here?"

"This is my morning for literacy testing, Jake. I told

you that last night. Besides, I know this boy. I tested him last week."

The mayor had his nose in the window like she was his girlfriend. "Judianne, it's not safe here. The shooter is right there in the cafeteria."

"Don't say shooter, Mayor Mashburn," Judianne said. "We're not on television. His name is Darrell. He has a third grade reading level, but he's smart. He may be ADHD, too. Let me talk to him." She swung open the door and stepped out of the truck.

Jake grabbed her shoulders. Judianne bridled. "Look, Jake. He's little. I'm little. One of you big mooses goes in there, he's likely to shoot you in the nose. I was with him just last week, talking. I've got rapport. He told me he likes comic books."

"All boys like comic books!" Jake forcefully turned her, and eased her back into the truck. "That boy has a gun, Judianne. Now git!"

Judianne started up the truck. "I guess I better tell you," she said softly to Jake, "WCAD has reports on this situation every fifteen minutes." Jake looked up and saw Danny Curtis, the WCAD reporter, coming out of the gym. Radio? Jake had thought a report in tomorrow's Courier would be his only problem. A cloud cover made the sky so dark the morning felt like evening.

Judianne drove out the drive far enough to be out

of sight, parked on the shoulder and walked back to the cafeteria. She'd bet dollars to donuts this was not the "hostage situation" the radio was promoting. The hunger for disaster in this town was just creepy, and the men were totally predictable. The more talk about shooters and hostages, the further the solution would slip out of Jake's control.

The younger of the deputies, Curly, was unrolling yellow crime scene tape along the tree line back of the cafeteria. "Hi, Curly," she called. "Jake wants me to see if I can negotiate."

The deputy frowned. Judianne smiled. "I know this kid," she said. The deputy nodded. Judianne slipped in the kitchen door. She stood quietly and listened—silence except for the hum of the refrigerators. The kitchen, still full of breakfast things and disinfectant smell, felt eerie with none of the hair-netted ladies in it. She slid into a narrow space between a refrigerator and the wall. "Hey, Darrell," she called, not too loud.

"Lena?" The muffled voice came from behind a door at the end of the kitchen.

"No, it's Judianne, the reading lady." She waited, but there wasn't another sound. On the door an open padlock hung on its hasp, so she guessed the door didn't lock from inside. Jake would want to know that. "I checked the drugstore for that Marvel Comic you like, 'Moon Knight.' Is that the one?" She waited, holding her breath.

Finally a soft, "Yeah. But I've got a gun now. Don't come in."

"Are you all by yourself in there?"

"None of your business."

Out in the yard, members of The Living God Church had started to arrive. Cars were parked at hurried angles along the shoulder of the road and the yellow crime scene tape was already tattered and pasted to the driveway.

"No, I don't know where the bathrooms are!" Jake yelled at a young guy. "This isn't a sporting event!" Jesus! What this was, was a nightmare. Reverend Pikestaff had evidently told his flock to meet at the flagpole, where the church members were becoming a huddled shifting bunch, those on the cafeteria side peeling off to hide behind the others, carrying the group past the flagpole and down the other side of the slope. Some had begun to pray on their own.

Jake knew he'd better take care of business pretty damn quick, but as he started toward the kitchen door a wild voice shrieked. "That's my grandbaby in there!" Jake darted back to the front to see a blond, heavy-set woman running across the yard. "Tiffani Casey. My granddaughter. She's the hostage!" The woman steadied herself on Jake's arm. "Somebody said she's in there. I want to go in there for her. Let me take her place. Oh, please, God. Let me be the hostage."

"How'd she get on to the grounds in the first place?"

"Her Daddy takes her to school after leaving off the milk and eggs for the kitchen here. Sometimes she walks from here."

"Who's her Daddy and where is he?"

"Bobby Casey from the dairy. Works afternoons at K-Mart. He doesn't even know she's missing."

Jake put his hand on the woman's shoulder. "I'm sorry about your granddaughter. If it works out you can go in and take her place, I'll let you. But right now, we don't know if Tiffani's really in there. Brian!" he called, "If you could take this good woman and get her a drink of water and stay in touch, I'll let you all know."

Overhead the whap, whap, whap of a helicopter filled the dark sky. Television. Shit!

The pantry shelves were heavy with institution-al-size cans of vegetables and boxes of generic corn flakes and pasta. Darrell said, "This here's Raynelle."

"Pleased to meetcha, Raynelle. My name's Judianne."

"Likewise," Raynelle said and leaned forward to extend a limp hand from the back corner, where she was lounging on a hundred-pound sack of potatoes, a pack of paper napkins for a pillow. Her hair was lank with dirt and grease, and her fingernails were gnawed and black around the edges. She didn't bother to put out the joint she was smoking. Darrell, a small guy, sat in the other corner on a huge can of lima beans. He was holding a large handgun. After introducing his hostage, he fidgeted.

"Listen Darrell, the Sheriff's here," Judianne began. "That's good news because he's a good guy, and he'll make it easy for you to just give me the gun and get on to class."

"How do we know this Sheriff is a good guy?" Raynelle asked casually. "How can we know he won't just clap us both in the pokey?"

"Gee, Raynelle. I'm getting the idea that you are not exactly the hostage here."

"Yes, she is!" Darrell said. "I forced her in here at gunpoint."

"Uh huh. And where'd you find such a handy hostage?"

"Darrell and I go way back," Raynelle volunteered and took another puff. "We were in foster care together last year until we got caught kissing. Just kissing, can you believe it? And bam! We both got shifted."

"We were lying down kissing," Darrell said. "On your bed."

"Yeah, whatever."

An exhaust fan up near the ceiling rattled but barely stirred the air in the pantry. "Look, you two. The clock's ticking. We need to wrap this up before others get involved. Now, the best thing would be for you to hand me the gun. Is it loaded?"

Darrell looked at the gun. "I think so. It's real heavy."

"Lemme see." Judianne stepped forward and reached for the gun, but Darrell pulled back and pointed it at her. "Point that thing at the floor!"

"No!" Darrell was shaking.

Judianne backed to the door and felt behind herself for the knob. "Tell you what, let me go talk to the Sheriff, and see if I can't make a deal."

"No way," Raynelle said. "If you leave here, the old sheriff will blow us up. Throw in tear gas at the very least. Huh uh," she said shaking her head. "You're staying right here."

Darrell steadied the gun and concentrated his face, squinting at her. Judianne took a deep breath of the stale air. No one said anything more. Raynelle lay back gazing at the ceiling, taking an occasional pull off the roach, but otherwise looking totally languid, like she was sunbathing. The minutes piled up, and the gun twitched in Darrell's hand but he didn't take his eyes off Judianne. Where was attention deficit when you needed it? Judianne sat down cross-legged and leaned her back against the door. The clatter of the fan kept her from being able to hear what was going on outside. If she yelled, could Jake hear her? Where the hell was Jake, anyway? Why wasn't he banging on the door, putting on the pressure, playing the bad cop? Surely, by now, he knew she was in here.

"How come you to show up here at the Center, Raynelle?" Judianne asked.

"I just dropped by to see my old friend Darrel." Raynelle had the rough, darkened skin of the homeless. She could be sixteen or thirty-five. She could have hitched here yesterday and stayed in a field last night. Maybe she traded sex to some guy for the weed.

Darrell had leaned his elbows on his knees, his arms undoubtedly about to give out with the weight of the gun. He craned his neck and circled his head like he was working out the kinks. Finally, he lay the gun in his lap and let himself slump on the can of lima beans. She hadn't told Jake, but this Darrell was the kind of hard luck case that always set her motherliness ablaze. She'd wanted to bring him home with her last week. She could teach him to read, for sure. And then, as she told all the kids, once you can read, the sky's the limit.

"I didn't mean to shoot that old woman," he said.

"Who did you mean to shoot?"

"Nobody! I ain't a killer."

"I know that, Darrell."

"How do you know?"

"It's in your palm."

"My what?"

"Last week when you came in to read for me, and

I saw all that spaghetti sauce on your hands. Remember me looking at your palm, right here. Remember?"

"I don't believe in that crap."

"There sure as hell weren't any killer lines."

"Do you really know the sheriff?"

"He's my boyfriend."

Raynelle perked up. "You're shitting me. How old are you?"

"This is the reading lady," Darrell said. "She's like a teacher."

"You look like a kid."

"I know. Everybody says that. Listen, Darrell, the sheriff and Mayor Mashburn have the idea you're holding Raynelle hostage."

"I am."

"What I'm saying is that this is a very dangerous situation. Okay? So the three of us need to go out together."

"Naw," Raynelle said, as she took a last puff and flipped the almost invisible leavings onto the floor. "We're just going to wait for the old gal to come back."

"What d'ya mean?"

"It wasn't nothing but a flesh wound. She didn't even want to go to the hospital. But the nurse made her go 'cause she's so old and has a bad heart."

"Where'd you get all this information, Raynelle?"

The girl sniffed and raised her hand as though to take a puff, then seeing she didn't have one, she lowered it.

"She'll tell Mr. Baird it was an accident," Darrell said. "She said she'd be right back."

"How'd you get in here, anyway?" Raynelle asked Judianne.

"It's a small town."

"It looks big through the fence," Darrell said.

"Well it's spread out. You could say that Cadillac is wide but not deep."

"You living with the sheriff?"

"Nope."

"You ever been married?"

"Once."

"That's what I want, to be married. My mom was too stupid to ever get anybody to marry her. She was just giving it away for free." Raynelle's lip twisted and one eye flickered like she might cry, but she got control of that real quick with a toss of her head. "Tell the old sheriff to put a ring on your finger or zip it up."

Darrell took a loud breath. "Down in Custer County, if they catch you with a gun, they try you as an adult and send you to a real prison. Little guys like me get raped every day. Every day."

"So let's make sure that doesn't happen to you."

"I'd rather die right here."

"For God's sake, you don't have to die or be raped. Just give me the gun."

Raynelle rose up on one elbow. "Lay off him, Judianne, he's learning to be a man."

"No, he's not."

"To get what men want, and we all know what men want, a guy's got to step up, got to prove he's a man. Right Darrell?" Raynelle lay back again, her legs straddling the potatoes, her back arched. "Right, Darrell?"

"I'm not going to talk to any sheriff!" he said.

Judianne leaned forward and glared at him. "Listen to me, you! You are a hard luck kid! I was a hard luck kid, too. And not too smart. I messed up my life good. Bad marriage to a jerk lawyer. Now I'm telling you, if you are lucky enough to get Jake Hale on your side, you better trust him."

"You and the sheriff aren't gonna have any brats, are ya?" Raynelle asked.

Judianne paused. Was there anything for sure she knew about her life? "Don't know," she said. She was forty and had laid off the pill ever since she'd started going with Jake in the spring. He said that was okay with him, and they both knew they were too old to be handing off to fate this way but that's what they'd been doing. She thought about this now as she watched the gun twitch in Darrell's hand, and she steadied herself, trying to count the days since her last period. How was Jake going to take this news?

"This is Mira Bartok, reporting from the Juvenile Detention Center in Cadillac with more on the Hostage Crisis." Jake jerked his head to see a television reporter, flooded with lights, project into her microphone.

After failing to persuade Pikestaff to get his people out of here and then using what he knew was undue force to turn away a hot dog vendor, Jake passed through the glare of the TV lights into the near darkness of the cloudy day to return to the kitchen door to see Fred there with Tiffani Casey's grandmother, her head on the deputy's shoulder.

"Get her away from here."

"You told me to guard this door. Then you told me to guard her."

"Where's Curly?"

"Putting the damned scene tape back up. Mr. Baird is helping him."

Jake took out his cell phone and dialed. While he listened to it ringing, a man in his late fifties stepped up, heavy rifle at his side, chest out, crew cut standing at attention.

"Sheriff Hale. Help has arrived."

"Don't you see that yellow tape? Get back over there!"

"I'm here to help."

"I'm on the phone." Jake ground his teeth. He always tried to be a patient man, but Godamighty! Hot

259

dogs, television, Christians!

"It looks like you're on hold," said the guy with the crew cut.

"I'm not on hold," Jake said. "It's ringing."

"I have two more sharp shooters with me. I figure we put one on top of the administration building, one on the cafeteria, and me over on that berm," Crew Cut said. He nodded back to the rise on the edge of the playing field.

Jake lowered his phone. "Who the hell are you?"

"Alvin Debbs. You've seen me. I'm a citizen of Cadillac."

"Yeah, I've seen you, but under what authority are you bringing in armed men to what is already a very dangerous situation?"

"Do you have any idea what could happen here?" Debbs lifted his chin like he was talking to a moral inferior. "Do you remember what happened in Atlanta, that judge shot in his own courtroom, a deputy killed, a getaway right out in public."

"Yeah, Debbs, I remember. This is not Atlanta. We do not have a rapist going on trial here."

"You have a shooter who is surrounded by an unarmed crowd," Debbs said. "A desperate gunman who has already killed someone."

"No one has been killed."

"But if the law-abiding public had been armed in

Atlanta, any one of them could have picked off that bastard before he ever got down the courthouse steps."

Jake pressed the phone to his ear and turned away, holding his hand over his other ear. "I could have saved those lives," Debbs said, his strident voice growing louder. "Maybe drawn my pistol right there in the courtroom the moment he tried to disarm the escorting deputy."

Jake whirled around and spoke through gritted teeth. "The deputy wasn't supposed to be armed. It was a breakdown in protocol right there. If the police had followed the rules, that rapist never would have gotten a gun."

"Sheriff Hale," Debbs voice sounded almost gentle, "I hope you aren't depending on protocol to solve this crisis? You are short-handed. You need us."

Jake stepped forward, and Debbs took a step back.

"Is that one of your men I see up on top of the administration building? You get him down and all three of you take your guns home. I'll put you and your buddies in jail if you don't get the hell out of here."

"This gun is registered and their guns are registered, and we have a right to be any place we choose." Debbs about-faced and left, maintaining more dignity than Jake felt he'd been able to hang onto. He closed his phone. The grandmother was gone.

Fred shrugged. "Tiffani, the granddaughter, showed up. I guess she was just skipping school. You trying to reach Judianne?"

"Why would I be calling her in the middle of all this?"

"Because she's in there." Fred was silent for a second as he and Jake stared at each other. "Curly said you told Judianne to go in there and negotiate?"

Jake grabbed Fred by the collar. "Shit for brains!"

"I'm sorry," Fred squeaked.

"We don't know what kind of kid that is. He could be a psychopath for all we know. A rapist." Fred's pale freckled face grew dark. Jake let him go and wiped his hand down his own face to dry the sweat. He took his gun out of the holster and ducked into the kitchen.

Judianne had been braiding her own hair to help wait out the minutes. She checked her Timex. "You know, it was a good idea to wait for Lena to get here and straighten everything out, but they just may keep her overnight. Or, knowing Cadillac General, she could still be in the waiting room. I agreed to wait another ten minutes for her to come back. But once time is up, you're going to give me the gun, right? And I'm going to take it out to Jake. Raynelle, you'd better go with me so Jake and the mayor will know you're okay.

Jake could see the pantry door straight ahead. He listened. He thought he picked up a faint smell of marijuana and felt an ounce of relief. How bad could this be?

Keeping out of sight, he sidestepped along the front cafeteria wall, and, standing behind a curtain, checked things in the yard. From his years of counting crowds at football games he would put this bunch right about seven hundred. In a semi-circle behind the yellow tape, as far as he could see from side to side, people covered the yard and the field.

Jake held his breath and listened. In the gravel on the flat roof overhead, he heard footsteps and knew it was Reverend Pikestaff going up on the mountain to lead his flock, but he was surprised to hear the voice come over a bullhorn: "Let us pray."

As the television lights bathed them, the crowd bowed their heads and raised their arms to Heaven. Reverend Pikestaff's voice was deep and full for such a slight man, and his phrases rang out from Jake's boyhood. "Rain down your everlasting mercy."

And why the hell shouldn't they pray. He'd completely lost control of this catastrophe. The deep voice of the preacher reminded him of his father's friends—a solid rank of manhood that had awaited him while he grew up. But where were they today when he needed them? Dead or senile. Only Sloane Willard had survived with his brain and conscience intact. And now he was gone. Pikestaff was a leader. He'd built a gigantic church out there on the highway with closed circuit television to handle the overflow crowds, but he wasn't a guy—not one to cover your back. The other minister, the one in gym shorts, was a solid man, but he had left half an hour ago to escort a fainting girl to the hospital. What a waste. Jake knew what had to be done, but he was not a weighty man like his father, a man others obeyed.

He automatically bowed his head. "Heavenly Father," he whispered, "just her. Out safe. That's all I ask." He heard more footsteps coming onto the roof. Probably one of Debbs's men with his big rifle. Now his own breath shuddered as he realized he felt outnumbered. Two guns inside. Three guns outside. Jake wished now for the National Guard or the Cavalry or Angels — some righteous, restraining force.

Out on the edge of the crowd Jake saw the blinking light of an ambulance. Reverend Matthews, still in his gym clothes, got out and began pushing his way through, trying to get around people who had their eyes closed and their arms outstretched. Curly, doing something right for a change, ran to meet him and pulled him through the crowd. Jake reholstered his gun, left the kitchen and ran around to the front.

Matthews panted. "Sheriff, I've got real bad news. Lena Brandt is dead of a heart attack. She was well loved, a member of my church. There may be a reaction in the crowd when — "

Jake nodded and took out his phone. "State Police? This is Sheriff Hale of Ellis County. I have a class four emergency . . . You've heard. Good. Can you send me some black and whites and at least twenty men?" . . . Well can you send me ten? . . . Jesus, can you send me three old ladies and a cripple!" He slammed the phone shut and threw it as far as it would go over the building, high, high, a fly into the outfield. God help me!

The crowd could be heard echoing the close of the prayer: Amen and Hallelujah, Sweet Jesus. But now they began to shout and applaud and whoop.

"Time's up, okay? Darrell, after I hand over the gun, I'll come back in to get you. Jake and I'll stay with you while you talk to Mr. Baird. Okay?"

With eyes to the floor Darrell handed over the heavy gun. Raynelle, still lying on the potatoes, let out a long, loud sigh. "I knew you'd wimp out in the end."

Darrell hung his head. Judianne spoke softly to him. "I'll just go get Jake. Everything's looking up now." She opened the pantry door. The rush of fresh air was thrilling. She had the gun. Nobody was going to get hurt. She let herself take in two deep breaths in celebration, then called, "Hey, Fred. Fred?" She looked out the back through the trees. Cars were parked every which way as far as she could see down the drive. Someone was on the roof with a bullhorn. Where had all these people come from? She turned back to the kids in the pantry.

"Listen, guys. I don't know what's going on, but I

think I better find Jake before we make any fast moves. He's nowhere out back. You all stay here. Don't show yourselves at the windows." She began to crawl across the cafeteria toward the front door. The gun in her hand clanked along the concrete floor. She shoved it in her jeans and kept low until she made it to the front door. There was a mass of people praying in the yard and out onto the field, multitudes like something in the Bible. She saw Jake back at the kitchen end of the building. He pulled back his arm and threw his phone high into the air.

"Jake! Jake!" She began to run toward him shouting. "It's all over. I've got the gun."

"Judianne!" he yelled. The crowd suddenly whooped and broke through the yellow tape to surround her and lift her onto their shoulders like a winning quarterback, the beneficiary of their prayer, exalted on high. "No! Wait!" she screamed, but the crowd was roaring. Their prayers had been answered, and they were headed up the hill to the flagpole.

Jake ran into the crowd, pushing and shoving against this convergence of the two greatest traditions in Cadillac, football and religion. She twisted and reached out her arms to him across the crowd. They carried her farther away, a kid in braids, face bleached by the television lights. He heard the pop of a gun. All his fears burst in his chest and tears blurred the sight of her as he watched her, like a flag losing its breeze, sink below the heads of the mob who marched her around the flagpole.

Alvin Debbs, stationed up on the berm, was far away, though he could tell that the girl had escaped. This was no time to let down his guard. With the eye of a steady, vigilant parent, he had watched the windows of the cafeteria as the crowd had grown gigantic and now went wild. His own beliefs and ideas of heaven were a tangle, but he was clear about his life here on earth and his place as a man in this country. There was a killer inside that building, but all these people could leave themselves wide open by lifting their arms and closing their eyes because he was there, well armed and on high ground.

And when the bastard finally showed his face at the cafeteria window, he got him right in the forehead.

"This is Mira Bartok. I'm still here reporting from the grounds of the Ellis County Juvenile Detention Center. The people are still leaving. It is taking hours on this dark and dreary day for all the cars to exit the single access road to the highway. The Sheriff's deputies have held back the crowd so that the ambulances could get in and out before these record-setting numbers began to get in their cars. Sheriff Jake Hale still declines to be interviewed, so we don't know yet what transpired inside the cafeteria. The new medical examiner is awaiting a forensics report on the bullet that wounded Lena Brandt. That bullet was located embedded in a doorframe of the Sugar House we mentioned earlier. We have no confirmation on that unofficial report that said it could have been from the same gun that killed Judianne McCall.

"That will be no surprise to all of us who have been watching the unfolding of this tragic story which began in the early morning with the wounding of Lena Brandt, an aide at the Juvenile Center for thirty-six years. Ms. Brandt died at Cadillac General Hospital of a heart attack after being wounded by Darrell Sturm. Interviews with some of the youths here attest to Ms. Brandt's great size and physical strength. Some boys said they were afraid of her, but as one boy put it, 'She was on our side.' Melvin Baird, director of the Center, said, 'Lena will be sorely missed. She ran the Sugar House, a snack place for the kids. She was going to retire this year.'

"The second victim was hostage Judianne McCall, former wife of prominent lawyer, Gavin McCall. She was a reading specialist who came to the Center once a week. All we know at this time according to Chief of Surgery, Arthur Woodall, is that she suffered massive blood loss from a wound to the upper thigh. As far as it can be explained tonight, the seriousness of her wound must not have been understood when she escaped the cafeteria and was hoisted onto the shoulders of the crowd and paraded around the flagpole. The gun has not been found. Judianne McCall died in the arms of those who had prayed for her.

"A second hostage, Raynelle Watkins, 17, was found by Deputy Fred Welcher in the kitchen pantry. 'Her grueling hours of trauma left her in a mute state,' he said.

"The shooter, Darrell Sturm, was a recent transfer to the Ellis County Detention Home from Custer County. He was being held on a drug charge. No one has come forth with any information about how he obtained the gun that killed Judianne McCall and wounded Lena Brandt. Sturm was downed by Alvin Debs, a decorated sharpshooter who had served as a U.S. Army Sergeant in Vietnam.

"It's now raining pretty steadily here in Cadillac, which has slowed the progress of the cars driven by people who came to the scene of this tragedy to pray for a happy outcome."

That night, alone in his house, Jake sat in front of the small, dark television. He and Judianne had kept their romance quiet. They went out to dinner and the movies, but Jake had never confided to anyone in town how deep he was into wanting this woman, so there was no one to rush to comfort him. Not that any of his buddies were the kind of men who'd know what to say to him tonight.

Automatically, he started to get a beer from the

fridge. But he was afraid of falling and fell back onto the couch. He knew where to look for the gun that had blasted a point blank hole in Judianne's thigh. After the shot she must have dragged it out of her pocket and let it drop, to be trampled into the mud by hundreds of shoes, the same mob so full of their righteous cheering, no one heard the pop, so exhilarated to have shouldered a woman they thought they'd rescued, they weren't careful with her. Damn them all.

He covered his face with his hands and let his head drop back onto the couch. She had become the focus of every plan, every fantasy, every hope he had for his best self. He had wanted to be a better man for her, to step into her dreams, to work beside her taking care of this kid and that kid, bucking them up, trying to give them some hope.

But everything that had happened since getting that call from Baird this morning, said he wasn't up to being a leader. He was a lightweight, a man no one would follow. But in Judianne's dreams he was the model for her students, the one they would look up to and pattern themselves on. She'd said he would be their hero.

§

Hillary O'Brian's
Cadillac Voices

I've been holding onto this piece ever since the death of Sloane Willard. Perhaps I wanted to keep for myself this message from a man I admired for his intelligence and moral courage. I took this Voice from the drawer again this morning and knew I should share it.

TREES

This spring my town seems to be filled with more yearning than usual—not just our chronic thirst to preserve the spirit of Oklahoma's gloried hell-for-leather past—but a deep hunger for a past we imagine other Americans to have had. Cadillac is yearning for an ice cream parlor.

From what I read in *The Courier* this dreamed-of establishment would be the centerpiece of a town green shaded by ancient elms and willows. Perhaps the ladies will carry parasols, and the carefree children will all wear white.

Like many of man's ambitions, this dream is not only out of time but out of place. Although our man-made ponds and lakes have manufactured a sticky humidity, the drizzly damp that

271

nurtures forests is limited to Oklahoma's eastern regions. We are in the west, Dust Bowl territory, with spirit-killing droughts in our past and undoubtedly in our future.

In spite of this, I am on the side of the dreamers. I grew up in Cadillac. My summer job was pedaling a bicycle through merciless heat to make grocery deliveries. What a splendid image a tree-shaded ice cream parlor would have been to the crazed and sweaty adolescent I was.

If only I had planted the trees then, sixty-five years ago. It would take that long and more water than it took to float the ark to grow the shade envisioned for a town green. So plant now. Water generously. Don't let the inevitable droughts stunt the saplings. Close the swimming pools if you have to. Let the lawns die. Plant now. Plant for your grandchildren. Plant for theirs. Make an oasis in the heart of Cadillac. A refuge, a park, a place to play and fall in love.

I would not like to live in a town that had no dreams, even ones so gingerbread as this. In this old lawyer's opinion, it is dreams that keep a place from being merely what it is.

Sloane Isaac Willard